Treaty Brides

THE SUBSTITUTE BRIDE

SAMANTHA CAYTO

The Substitute Bride
ISBN # 978-1-80250-523-8
©Copyright Samantha Cayto 2023
Cover Art by Kelly Martin ©Copyright March 2023
Interior text design by Claire Siemaszkiewicz
Pride Publishing

Published in 2023 by Pride Publishing, United Kingdom.

Collections
Rules of Summer: In the Heat of the Dungeon
Dark and Deadly: Dream Demon
S.W.A.L.K.: His True Heart
His Harem: Room for Elijah

THE
SUBSTITUTE
BRIDE

Dedication

To Desiree Holt, my mentor and friend. I shall miss you more than I have words to express.

Chapter One

"This is so unfair!"

Carwyn watched helplessly as his dear cousin Nora, Duchess of Windham and Countess of Kenworth, raged against her fate while pacing her private garden.

"How can the king and my father do this to me? After all they promised, I'm to be traded away like a prize cow to a foreign prince now that I'm of legal age to wed."

Carwyn had given up trying to keep pace with the furious girl. Her longer legs, fueled by anger, gave her an advantage. The best he could do was catch her attention with each turn leading back to his spot by the fountain. "They're scared, Nora. This alliance with the Southern Chain is critical to bolstering a defensive line against the Swarm, as well as to find their source and defeat them."

Nora turned furious eyes at him. "Ridiculous! The king is afraid of no one — and neither is my father."

Carwyn knew better than to argue the point, but he could vividly recall the time when his cousin had come down with the pox and nearly died from it. The look in her father's eyes was one of pure terror. No one was above being frightened — no one sane, anyway. And the Swarm was an enemy unlike any other. The mysterious people came from the gods knew where, completely destroying the places they attacked, killing, looting and burning everything and dragging those still alive away to an unknown fate — slavery probably, which was bad enough, but there were rumors of strange rituals and blood-drinking. He shivered at the mere thought of it, although his wiser self told him those were likely tall tales. At least he hoped so.

He chased after Nora's back and taking her arm, pulled her up short. "Please, Nora, calm yourself." When she turned her blazing gaze on him, he reminded himself that this was his liege lady as well as his kinswoman and friend. Swallowing back his urge to apologize, he pressed forward with telling her of the decision he'd come to only that morning. "I understand how hard it's going to be for you to make your home in a distant land. That's why I'm coming with you. If you'll have me, of course."

Letting go, he took a step back and braced for her response. Nora didn't like being 'handled', and what he was suggesting had to be embraced as her idea more than his. He ignored the unease manifesting in his queasy stomach. He'd only just arrived at the Moorcondian capital, a life-long dream of his. Kenworth was beautiful, quiet and...boring. His eighteenth birthday had given him the courage to press his parents once more to let him come visit the king's court and hopefully find a useful role there. They hadn't wanted to let their youngest child go so far away. Although they hadn't said as much, he knew his family worried that he was too delicate of mind and emotions to navigate court life. How much worse would they feel finding out that he'd sailed away to a distant land to live among strangers they knew little about?

Nora's high dudgeon eased, leaving a sheen of tears in her eyes. "You'd do that? Oh Carwyn, you know nothing of these Chainers. You don't understand how much your life would be different from what you're used to."

Carwyn swallowed his trepidation. "Neither do you. The traders who've been there say it's spectacular and the people are friendly." They also said the 'Chainers' were a fierce tribe of near savages. There was no point in bringing up that information, however. He took Nora's hands in his own. "And we'll have each other. If our childhoods taught us nothing else, together we are nearly invincible."

Nora surprised him with a tight embrace. "Oh Carwyn, your parents will be grief-stricken at the idea. They will never allow it. It's bad enough that Cariad is out to sea mapping those treacherous waters."

"That's different. What he's doing is inherently dangerous." Carwyn nevertheless took a moment to worry about his older brother. The bookish boy was ill-suited for such an adventure, but he was a wizard in memorizing topography and an excellent draftsman to boot. "And it's not for my parents to say. If the king decides I should go, then the matter is settled. If you ask him, I'm sure he will agree, if only because your father will advocate it. He wouldn't want you to be alone in this, Nora, and a whole army of maids at your side will never match the benefit of having a family member with you."

Nora let go and stepped away from him. She twisted her fingers as she spoke. "I shouldn't be so selfish, but I lack the courage to refuse your kind offer."

Carwyn put on a bright smile. "It's a plan, then. And who knows? Perhaps I'll find a lover of my own. It's past time I do so, and I have heard the Chainer men are gorgeous." He fluttered his eyelashes.

Nora chuckled as he'd intended. "Remember how we used to dream of what our first lover would be like? I never thought I'd go to my marriage bed a virgin. What if he's not kind to me?" As powerful as she was, Nora had the same worries and desires as anyone else of their age.

Carwyn clasped her arms and peered into her still-moist eyes. "Then we'll find a way to castrate the bastard and toss his genitals into the sea."

Nora rolled her eyes. "Well, if anyone can pull that off, it's you, Carwyn."

Before he could further soothe her fears, the heralds blared loudly. They both looked in the direction of the main entrance to the city. The Southern Chain prince had arrived. *Kai Aleki.* The Chainers had different titles. Once they were wed, Nora would be known as a kailisa as well as a princess, a duchess and a countess. He understood how important it was to her to have her own titles. The Chainers might not care about her independent positions. Becoming known only as an extension of her husband would grate on her. As a mere lord and not his father's heir, he could only relate to her feelings on the matter academically. In his more wistful moments, he wished he could become like Prince Ronan — the adored wife of a powerful man. If he went with Nora, his dream could never be, probably. The Chainers customs were not well known. It was possible that his attraction to men would be frowned upon…or even illegal. If he thought about it too much, he might go back on his offer. *Never.* Sacrificing for the royal family had been bred into him, and being Nora's champion had been his role in life for as long as he could remember.

Nora took in a shuddering breath. "He's arrived."

"Yes, and we must both get ready for the welcome banquet. Come… I'll walk you to your apartment." He took his cousin's hand and tugged her along. Whether she knew it or not, Nora was literally dragging her feet.

He deposited her with her maids, giving her a quick kiss on the cheek before leaving. "Make yourself as stunning as always, and Kai Aleki's eyes will pop out right in front of the court. You can do this," he added in a voice only for her ears.

Having done his duty, Carwyn hurried to his less luxurious accommodations in the palace. As a minor member of the king's extended family, he was entitled to be housed there, although he had to share. As he entered the room, two of his three roommates were entwined on a bed, flushed and puffing from their recent exertions. He paid them no mind. Those two were always going at it. He couldn't understand why they were so enthralled with one another. Boys his own age didn't interest him in the least. He wanted a man, someone strong enough to take charge and carry him off to bed. There was nothing arousing about holding on to a body as slender as his own. Carwyn craved muscle that could both mount him vigorously and be careful of him, too. *Is there such a man even out there for me?*

Heading for his own bed, he contemplated how he might style his hair. It was long enough to produce a decent braid and it would be a more formal look than leaving it down. He did love the feel of it swinging against his cheeks, but he wasn't in Kenworth anymore. He needed to blend into palace life and represent his family well. His small chest of drawers held fewer outfits than he would have liked, and there was really only one that would do for such an occasion. The green velvet tunic and trousers with gold thread trim brought out the green in his hazel eyes and complemented his yellow hair. He laid them carefully on top of his bed and stripped off what he was wearing. The other boys started making noises that indicated they weren't done with each other.

Carwyn *tsk*ed. "You'd best move your pretty asses. Princess Eleanora's betrothed has arrived." That news got them moving. They nearly tumbled onto the floor in their haste to leave the bed. Carwyn shook his head. At the same time, he admired how they'd been so engrossed in each other that they hadn't heard the heralds. Such devotion was enviable. Still, there was no time to dwell on such matters. "And I need someone to braid my hair, please."

* * * *

Carwyn arrived in the king's enormous receiving room in time to witness the royal family enter. His status rated a spot near the dais where the king already sat, his queen by his side. It gave him an up-close view of Nora's face. Her expression was aloof, something he knew she'd cultivated to mask her feelings. Her father's emotions were more on display. The man held his wife's hand with a hard look that made clear to all how much he hated what was happening. The Duchess of Vostguard looked sad, which wasn't surprising. The Marsher boy was a very empathetic person—or so Carwyn had heard. He didn't know Taryn very well, having spoken to him only twice for brief moments, but the man seemed very open and caring, embracing his husband's four daughters as if they were his own. Carwyn thought the influence Prince Soren's wife had on him was a good thing, and he hoped they never lost that bit of humanity.

Everyone's attention was grabbed by a yell that made Carwyn jump. He trained his gaze along with the rest of the court on the double doors opening. His mouth dropped at what he saw. A dozen men entered, wearing nothing more than colorful skirts draped over their narrow hips to hang below their knees and calf-high black boots. Their bare chests bore strange patterns, as did their faces. Each man had black hair tied into a knot on the top of his head. There was utter silence as the Moorcondians of the royal court got their first look at the Southern Chain warriors. Then there was another startling cry before the men came into the room in a synchronized crouch of three rows. They chanted as one in a language that Carwyn had never heard before. Each word was punctuated by sharp arm movements that included slapping their thick thighs. As they progressed toward the dais, their actions were in perfect unity, except for their expressions. Each man contorted his face in different ways, all shows of menace and threats of violence that made Carwyn glad these were Moorcondia's allies, not enemies. When the first row was only a few feet from the dais, they halted, again as one, and taking a knee, swiveled their heads back toward the doors, their palms pressed together in front of their chins, heads bowed.

That's when the most impressive one of them all stepped into the room. Kai Aleki wasn't the tallest or brawniest of the Chainers, yet he nevertheless commanded everyone's attention. Like his men, he wore only a skirt that wrapped around his tapered waist. As he walked, Carwyn caught flashes of the man's muscular thighs. His glossy black hair was also tied into a knot on the top of his head, but the real attraction was his beautiful face. Carwyn's breath caught at the sight of it. He'd never set eyes upon a more beautiful man in his whole life. Aleki was the perfect example of his peoples' appearance, with his gold-hued skin and dark eyes that turned up slightly at the outer corners and highlighted by slashing cheekbones. His only face-markings, however, were vine-like patterns that climbed up along his temples. It was all the more attention-grabbing for its subtlety. And unlike his men, the kai made no sound and kept his face neutral as he approached the king, his gaze fixed on his destination. When he reached the front row of his men, he stood in the middle of them, pressed his palms as they did and bowed his head to the king. The show of respect lasted only a second before he straightened and stood with his arms crossed and legs braced.

Now Carwyn's view was only of the man's profile, but that was enough to make his heart stutter and his cock harden. For the first time in his life, he was jealous of his cousin. Nora was going to have this pure example of masculinity in her bed. *Does she even appreciate him?* A glance at her face told him nothing. Her cool expression hadn't changed — nor had her father's. If anything, Carwyn could swear the prince's displeasure had ratcheted. The Duchess of Vostguard had placed his other hand over his husband's in an obvious effort to soothe him. His reaction wasn't hard to understand. Nora was a refined, scholarly woman who led a fairly quiet life of duty. Whatever other kind of man he might be, Aleki was the embodiment of raw power. Their lives together could be passionate if his cousin allowed herself to embrace that side of her. He wasn't sure she could, and for certain, her father was having a hard time with the idea that his daughter was going to be bedded by a man whose fierceness rivaled his own.

There was no more time to ponder Nora's fate, however. The king stood with raised arms. "Greetings, Kai Aleki, and welcome to Moorcondia." He held out one hand in Nora's direction, a silent command for her to approach. Being a dutiful niece and subject, she came to his side and took the proffered hand. "May I present Her Royal Highness, Princess Eleanora, Duchess of Windham and Countess of Kenworth." He paused a fraction of a second. "And your bride."

Aleki once again put his palms together and this time bowed to Nora. She inclined her head with downcast eyes. Neither of them spoke, not even rehearsed greetings that propriety normally dictated. Nora's silence was not surprising, but perhaps Aleki was equally unhappy with his fate. The moment of slight awkwardness passed, however, and when Aleki straightened and lowered his arms, his eyes slanted to one side. Carwyn jolted as his gaze and the kai's met. It was a brief encounter and over in the blink of an eye, yet in that time, Carwyn's desire for the man caused him to get hot and breathless. His palms grew moist, and his mouth dropped open on a sigh that he couldn't hold back. Aleki showed no reaction other than a quick flaring of his nostrils before he turned his attention back to the king.

* * * *

The cool breeze of the Moorcondian night was a welcome respite from the stifling ballroom. Taking a moment to stretch his legs outside of the crowd helped Aleki digest the heavy meal he'd been served before the king and his courtiers had migrated into the adjacent larger room for dancing and lively conversation. He had no skill in either, unless one counted the baiting a warrior did to demonstrate his fierceness and the bragging with comrades after battle. Neither of those things were called for in this stilted, official affair. His host had obviously put on the best hospitality his country had to offer but Aleki couldn't wait to do his duty, seal the treaty and get back out to sea.

"My kai, you shouldn't be out here on your own. Your presence will be missed."

Aleki didn't spare his cousin a glance. Rei was like a fruit fly, always buzzing about demanding attention yet lacking an ability to sting. "It grew stuffy in there. I needed some fresh air...and peace. These Moorcondians chatter incessantly, like sea birds begging for scraps of fish. All except for my betrothed, of course, who has said barely two words to me all throughout dinner." He knew it was an unfair statement, given that he was equally unenthusiastic to make his bride's acquaintance—not that Rei would dare to point out such a thing.

"Yes, my kai. I understand your discomfort. Moorcondian buildings are very enclosed, no doubt because of their cold season. The far more temperate climes of our dear country should make for a lovely change for your kailisa. She will quickly come to appreciate her great fortune in marrying you."

Aleki merely grunted, unconvinced that Eleanora would ever feel more than resentment toward their marriage...and him. She was an obviously proud woman, as well she should be, given her status. She didn't need to say anything for him to understand her unhappiness toward her fate. Marriage meant leaving her place of birth, her family and her independent power. In the Chain, she would be no more than his position afforded her, which wasn't as much as she was used to. Finding an unmarried member of the royal family worthy of her hand hadn't been easy. It had come down to him and only him, given that all of his male relatives of marriageable age had wives already. His life-long disinterest in women had led him to this predicament. The irony of his situation was not lost on him.

"Perhaps," he allowed, although it was more out of politeness. "The young tend to be more adaptable." And she *was* young, too much so to his way of thinking, nearly half his age. He knew many men would find such a situation alluring. For him, it was one more obstacle to clear. A young, and likely inexperienced, bride would require great patience and care. He worried that he was not equipped to meet the challenge. He was a warrior after all, not a diplomat, and he had no experience ushering a woman into sex. He supposed the effort was not unlike that made for a man—not that he'd done much of that, either. He preferred his bed partners to be seasoned, enthusiastic and occasionally inventive. He feared that with

Princess Eleanora he would get exactly none of those things — not that he could blame her.

Clapping his hand on Rei's shoulder, he said, "Go back in and smooth my absence away, cousin, if it's even been noticed. I will return to the ballroom shortly."

Rei's expression showed his displeasure at that order, yet he knew better than to argue. Not only would it be impudent, but it would also be pointless. Aleki wasn't easily persuaded or cowed by anything, let alone a sense of decorum. With a quick bow over his pressed palms, Rei left him, which was all to the better when his leaving gave Aleki a clear line of sight to the opposite end of the balcony. A young man had come out to stand by the railing, his pretty, flushed cheek and dreamy smile visible from Aleki's vantage point. Now here was a Moorcondian that he actually wanted to talk to. He silenced his inner warning system that he was heading into trouble and crossed the space between them.

"Good evening."

The boy jerked, obviously startled. As a warrior of the Chain, Aleki knew how to move silently, even on stone.

But the surprise at his approach quickly morphed into one of greeting, the boy's pretty, full lips curving up into a smile. He turned to Aleki and clasped his fingers under his chin to make his bow.

Charmed at the effort, Aleki grinned, then did something very stupid. Stepping closer, he reached out to take the boy's hands between his own. There was a sudden pop and sizzling along his skin, as if lightning had struck the lines of his ship. The sensation shot straight to his cock, making his small clothes tight. He was glad to have donned them, a suggestion of Rei's for modesty's sake that he'd discounted before. Not now. The last thing he needed was to tent his kilt in front of his hosts.

His own reaction hardly mattered anyway. The boy's eyes went wide, and a puff of breath passed his lips. Aleki wasn't the only one affected by the touch. He worked to hide his reaction and did what he'd intended to do by tugging the boy's fingers away from each other and pressing his palms together. "It's like this." Having completed his lesson, he forced his feet to take two steps back.

With a coy look, the Moorcondian repeated his bow, a flawless execution made with delightful grace and smooth politeness. "Good evening, Kai Aleki. I trust you are enjoying the ball."

"Indeed, but I grew warm and needed some air." He made his own bow, pleased by how his brief respite had turned into something far more interesting and pleasurable.

"Oh. I fear I'm not worthy of that type of greeting from you."

Aleki studied the boy's expression, utterly charmed at the statement. *So naïve, yet enticing in the extreme.* "It's a gesture of respect, not subservience. All are worthy of it, from our prima kailisa to the peasants who till the fields."

"Really?" The boy dropped his gaze, then peeked at him from under his lashes. "There is so much to learn about your culture."

"I will be happy to teach you." Even as he made the offer, he felt a sudden sadness of how short his time in Moorcondia would be. "I'm afraid I don't know your name."

"I'm Lord Carwyn of Kenworth." The boy sketched a deep bow in the fashion of his people. "No one of importance, sir."

Aleki crossed his wrists behind his back because the temptation to touch this Lord Carwyn was too great. "You are being modest, surely. Your place in the reception room and during the banquet indicates otherwise."

Carwyn shrugged his slender shoulders, making his long, braid dance. "I'm a cousin to the king, that is all. If my parents and older siblings were in attendance, I would have been lost in the crowd of courtiers, to be sure." He smiled again, showing two adorable dimples.

Aleki wanted to lick each one with his tongue. He forced himself to make polite small talk instead. While he did, it would keep the boy in front of him. "We are kindred spirits, then, as I am cousin to the prima kailisa, not the closest one. Even my advisor, Rei, is closer in relation to her, yet I am the only eligible one. She hopes that I am deserving of King Auden's niece."

Carwyn giggled, an almost musical sound. "Have no worries on that account, sir. You are an impressive man. Everyone can see that, especially after your amazing introduction." He paused, and his tongue flicked out to touch his lower lip. "May I ask what your men were saying and doing as they preceded you?"

"You may ask me anything you like. My warriors displayed our traditional chants, gestures and facial expressions my people have been employing for countless generations to demonstrate our ferocity to our enemies. It is meant to impress. Did it?" he couldn't help asking.

Carwyn's gaze did a slow down-then-up perusal of Aleki's chest before answering. "Yes." The one word

Samantha Cayto

was said in a breathless tone, and his cheeks pinked, easily seen given his pale skin.

"I'm gratified."

"I think you knew the answer to your question already...sir," he added with another coy look.

"Call me Aleki."

Now Carwyn's eyes widened. "I couldn't possibly do so. We may be similar in positions in our family trees, but you are far above my station, given your status as the master of the Chain's fleet."

Aleki briefly wondered how hard it would be to convince the boy to say his name in bed, then dismissed the notion. He was there as the intended groom of the king's niece. And while he knew the Moorcondians would have no problem with his choice of bedmate, lying with anyone other than the princess would be a damnable insult. He sighed inwardly and ground his teeth at his predicament. Then again, but for his betrothal, he would never have met this fetching boy. The encounter at least had the benefit of a pleasant diversion. Looking and some conversations were going to have to satisfy him, however.

"I consider my station to be one of highest service to my people, not of privilege. But I understand court decorum. Please call me 'kai', at least."

"Kai." Carwyn pressed his palms together and made a perfect bow. "I think my cousin Nora will be looking for me now, so I should return to the ball."

Aleki cocked his head at this new information. "You two are particularly close?"

"Yes, kai, we are. We have been fast friends since childhood. In fact, I will accompany her to the Southern Chain."

Aleki's heart skipped a beat at the news. At the same time, he knew he was in deep trouble. How could he manage to keep his hands off this beautiful boy if he saw him every day? Being a consummate warrior, he let nothing of his thoughts show, however. Instead, he fell back on studied politeness. "How delightful. I look forward to hosting you in my humble home."

"Thank you." Carwyn's expression turned pensive. "I appreciate your welcome." He glanced up at Aleki, and in those bright green and gold eyes, Aleki saw something akin to...fear? Of what, though? The unknown? Perhaps, or maybe like himself, the Moorcondian lord was realizing that their proximity could be dangerous.

Chapter Two

"This is the private garden of the royal family." Nora gave a sweeping gesture with her arm, a lackluster effort. "It's not as impressive as the formal ones, but I've spent many happy times here with my parents and sisters."

One didn't need to know the woman as well as Carwyn did to hear the sadness in her tone. Nora hadn't been giving her intended a tour of the palace with much enthusiasm as it was. Now, she had clearly reached her limit. Carwyn knew it was time to act as the buffer he intended to be. "You are tired, your highness. No surprise, given how long the ball lasted." Not that Nora had stayed for all of it. "Perhaps a nap before taking tea with the dowager queen is in order?" He punctuated the suggestion with a bright smile.

No fool she, Nora jumped at the chance for an escape. Putting the back of her hand to her forehead, she said, "You're right, Carwyn, as always. It wouldn't do to visit Great-Grandmother with droopy eyes." She flashed an almost smile at Aleki. "If you will excuse me? Carwyn can complete the outing, with your permission of course. Perhaps a tour of the rest of the grounds is tedious for a warrior such as yourself."

"Not at all. Your home is most impressive and unlike anything in my experience. Lord Carwyn's company is quite enjoyable. I'm sure he'll keep me entertained." He bowed to her. "I look forward to taking tea with you and the dowager queen later this afternoon."

The man was more modestly dressed this day, with a loose tunic of dark green belted by a thin rope covered in small shells. It hung past his narrow hips to mid-thigh. His kilt, as he now knew they called it, had a colorful pattern in various shades of green. Somehow, the covered chest was more alluring. Carwyn had found himself trying to get a peek at it through the V of the shirt as they'd walked around the palace. His behavior had been most inappropriate, yet he was powerless to stop it. Since their brief contact on the balcony, he hadn't been able to get the man out of his thoughts — and dreams. He'd woken sweaty and sticky that morning, his head filled with all kinds of fantasies. Promising to accompany Nora to the Southern Chain had either been the best idea he'd ever had or the worst. He could only hope that some other Chainer warrior caught his fancy once they arrived. Otherwise, living in Aleki's household would be torturous.

Carwyn was forced to get out of his own head when Nora hurried away with a swish of her skirts, her two maids trailing behind her and trying to keep up. For a tired woman, the princess was leaving with a lot of energy, and Aleki was watching her with knowing eyes. Carwyn stepped into his line of sight. "Shall we continue, kai? There is a lovely fountain just beyond the hedgerow."

Aleki didn't hesitate to switch his attention. His stare was unnerving. "That sounds intriguing, but I wonder if we might sit over there for a short while." He pointed to the gazebo frequented by Nora's family in particular.

"Of course." Carwyn didn't hesitate to lead the man from behind, but as they entered the small structure, it seemed to be an awfully tight space, despite its open sides. He made a point to sit as far from Aleki as he could, even as he longed to jump into the man's lap. *Stop it!*

Aleki lounged bonelessly with his arms draped over the back of the bench. "Lovely." His gaze was on Carwyn, however, not the beautiful garden around them.

Carwyn cleared his throat delicately to dislodge the lump forming there. "It is. I had lunch with Nora and her family here the day after I arrived. It was great fun."

Aleki cocked his head, something he seemed to habitually do when he was about to ask a question. "I am curious, I must confess, about Prince Soren's wife."

Carwyn smiled. "Oh, the duchess. Yes, that is a bit unusual, isn't it?"

"And yet, everyone here appears to take the situation in stride—that a man can be a wife."

"The duchess makes it easy. He's such a nice, unassuming man. Nora and her sisters adore him and he them. At least, that's how it looks to me. And it is a love match, however their marriage started out." He couldn't help sighing wistfully. "Everyone should be so lucky to have a man look at them the way Prince Soren does his wife." Fearing he'd given too much of himself away, he glanced warily at the kai.

Aleki's heated gaze burned the gazebo's cool breeze away. "Is that what you wish for? Because you'll have plenty of admirers in my homeland if it is."

"Truly? Your people have no trouble with men lying together?"

Aleki threw back his head and laughed. "Given how much time my people spend at sea and how few of our sailors are women, we'd be hard pressed to object to something so commonplace."

"That's, um, good to know." Embarrassed and afraid that his desire for the man might show through his eyes, Carwyn dropped his gaze to pluck at a thread on his seat cushion. He nearly jumped out of his skin when Aleki came to sit down beside him. Honestly, the man moved more silently than anything Carwyn could even think of as an analogy.

"I'm sorry," the kai murmured. "Does my closeness disturb you?"

Carwyn felt his cheeks heat. "I think you know it does."

Aleki reached out to pluck strands of Carwyn's hair between thumb and forefinger. "You only have to ask, and I will move away."

"I think we both also know that's not going to happen." Sense warred with desire, however, and won. "But this is a very public place, at least to those who frequent the private quarters of the royal family, so…" He forced himself to his feet and took a step back. "How about I show you that fountain?"

Aleki rose with enviable grace. "How about you show me the closest blind spot in this garden?" He chuckled in the next instant and shook his head. "I'm being very disrespectful of your cousin. Please forgive my boorish behavior."

"I honestly don't think she'd mind—relieved, more likely, that I've captured your attention." Carwyn nearly clapped his hand over his mouth with that intemperate observation.

Aleki chuckled. "Don't worry. You aren't telling me anything I don't already know myself. Princess Eleanora has no more enthusiasm for our impending marriage than I do. But duty demands the sacrifice. The Swarm has to be stopped." Leaving the gazebo, he started down the path that would lead them to the larger formal gardens—and past a pretty, vine-covered pergola.

Carwyn was determined to ignore the lure of that place and hurried in the kai's wake. "We want to take the path to the left," he said, staying behind the man, because walking next to him on the narrowly placed gravel would allow their bodies to brush too close. Besides, the view of the man's backside, even draped in fabric, as well as the sight of his muscular calves, was highly entertaining. There was power there, and he couldn't help imagining what it would be like for it to be turned on him—in the most pleasurable way, of course.

He shouldn't have been surprised when Aleki headed directly through the opening of the pergola and walked to the very back of it. There was a swing there and the man sat on it. He laughed when it moved, clearly an unexpected consequence. "What is this?" Even as he asked, he pushed at the ground with one foot to increase the motion.

Carwyn approached with his hands clasped behind his back and trying to look casual when his heart was beating a quick tempo. "It's a swing. Don't you have any in your homeland?"

"We swing on vines as children for fun but don't construct anything like this." He stopped it abruptly. "I shall have to have one crafted in my own garden when I return." Then he did the irresistible and patted the spot beside him. "Come join me."

With his gaze cast downward, Carwyn bit his lower lip before saying, "I don't think that is a good idea."

"Oh, it's most assuredly not. And I should show better judgment, but I can't muster any at the moment. No one can see us here, can they?"

"Noooo, but I'm not sure that's relevant. I love my cousin and want to be respectful of her."

"Admirable, and I intend to be respectful of her too, and faithful — once we are wed. That is not until tomorrow morning, and I would consider it an honor if you were to indulge me a little bit on this last day of my being an unmarried man." He held out his hand.

Carwyn was unable to resist the request. The fact that he knew Nora wouldn't care what he did with Aleki helped ease his conscience. And no one could see them, so she wouldn't be embarrassed at court. He let Aleki clasp his hand and draw him down onto the swing.

"This is delightful, is it not?" Aleki asked as he set the seat in motion once more. He didn't release his hold on Carwyn, electing instead to turn his arm in order to kiss the inside of his wrist.

That simple touch sent Carwyn's heart galloping, and his cock strained for freedom against his snug trousers. He stuttered out a breath before he could get words past his lips. "If you aren't careful, you'll make me come from such a simple touch."

Aleki smiled broadly. "That won't do. If I'm going to make you come, I want it to be from something far more passionate." That was all the warning he gave before hugging Carwyn close and kissing him.

All his previous experience had been mere youthful fumbling, a brief stop before getting down to more interesting activity. This kiss, however, was different. The way Aleki devoted his attention to claiming his mouth proclaimed it as an end in and of itself. The man sucked and nipped for long seconds before pressing his tongue for entrance. It explored with lazy thoroughness, leaving Carwyn breathless and eager for more. It was he who practically climbed onto Aleki's lap. And the man took the opportunity to clasp Carwyn's ass and squeeze. As he did so, Carwyn's eager cock brushed against Aleki's hard body, making him climax. The lack of control surprised him and left him shaking from the power of the release. He broke off the kiss and tucked his face into the side of Aleki's neck, both because of embarrassment and in an effort to get himself under control.

When he'd caught his breath, he scrambled to rectify the indiscretion. "That wasn't supposed to happen. It can never happen again."

The kai ran a soothing hand down Carwyn's back. "I won't apologize for giving you pleasure. I enjoyed it very much, and this is my last bit of freedom before duty binds me to your cousin. And you're right. It won't happen again." He gave a quick kiss to Carwyn's temple before moving him gently away.

The hard length of the man pressed against Carwyn's thigh. "Oh...but you haven't..." His cheeks heated as he stumbled over his words and realized he didn't know how to end the sentence. *Am I offering to make him come?* What a ludicrous and dangerous escalation that would be.

"Not to worry." Aleki had them both on their feet in the next instant. "I will tend to that problem when I make myself presentable to the dowager queen." He tucked a stray hair behind Carwyn's ear. "And I fear time has grown short. I will have to leave without seeing this amazing fountain. I find the dalliance I've had with you more than a sufficient substitute."

Aleki dropped his hold on him and walked out of the pergola. With unexpected sadness, Carwyn followed, no longer sure that traveling back to the Southern Chain with Nora was the best idea. Being near Aleki and not being able to touch him was going to be painful in many ways. How could he have foreseen that this exotic man would capture his attention so quickly and almost violently? And it wasn't only his dick responding in that manner. His heart was elbowing its way in there as well, and that was crazy. Love at first sight was a romantic notion for stories of fair maidens and noble warriors. It didn't happen in real life. *Does it?*

He rubbed his chest as if he could wipe the burgeoning feelings away. And as he walked into the brightness of the afternoon, he considered telling Nora that he wasn't coming with her after all. She'd be angry at his change of mind and worse, sad. He'd have to explain why, and that didn't seem fair, either. Nora's future shouldn't be compromised because of his wayward desires. Duty commanded him to stand firm against his attraction to the Chainer warrior. He just hoped the man would do the same. If not, life in the Southern Chain was going to be miserable.

* * * *

Aleki felt a line of sweat slide down the middle of his back under the frightening gaze of the dowager queen. The woman was as formidable as the prima kailisa. And that made him experienced in letting nothing of his feelings show as he sipped her surprisingly strong tea from a delicate cup. He understood this custom of eating something between dinner and supper, because Rei had schooled him in it. But nothing of the dainty sandwiches or oversweet cakes appealed to him, so he ate only as much as good manners dictated and kept his attention on his hostess and her questions. He appreciated how this matriarch of the royal family held sway and that she chose to scrutinize him in her own domain rather than with the crushing crowd of the court surrounding them. Here she had his undivided attention, and he dared not do anything to jeopardize the treaty. However much he disliked the idea of marrying a woman, the safety of his people demanded he do nothing to hinder what was best for them.

The princess yawned delicately next to him, something she'd been doing with some frequency, despite her purported nap. He suspected it was more out of boredom than sleepiness yet hoped that it would spur the dowager queen to end the tea soon. His hopes were dashed a moment later.

"*Nora.*" The dowager queen's tone was brusque. "You'll do no one any good if you are exhausted by the time of your wedding. Go back to your suite and get some rest before supper."

The princess practically slammed down her cup and jumped to her feet. "Yes, Great-Grandmamma, you are quite right as usual. I will take my leave." Turning to him, she added, "I look forward to seeing you at supper, Kai Aleki." She was well-trained. One might even think she was sincere. With that, she curtsied to them both and fled.

When Aleki put his own cup down in a bid to follow her, the dowager queen squashed that intent with a hard stare. He settled into his chair with as much nonchalance as he could muster, but he'd be damned if he'd swallow more tea. He was practically swimming in it already. Besides, if he gave himself too much time to think, his mind would wander back to the stolen moments with Carwyn in the lovely bower of tree limbs and flowers. The taste of the boy lingered on his tongue, no matter what he drank or ate. And if he didn't shove those thoughts aside, his body would embarrass him, regardless of how much his tunic and kilt covered his groin.

"You're not interested in marrying my great-granddaughter, are you?"

The question, which was more an accusation, caught him by surprise. "Madam, I..."

"Don't bother to lie." The woman waved her hand in dismissal. "I'm too old to fool and too experienced in the ways of people to believe otherwise."

Aleki picked his words carefully. "Princess Eleanora and I are newly introduced. It would be disingenuous of me to profess an affection that I cannot feel on such a short acquaintance." Even as he said those sensible words, an image of Carwyn popped into his head. *Desire and love might come that quickly to someone...with the right person.* He cut that train of thought off quickly. "I'm sure after time enough for us to know each other better, affection will come. She's a very intelligent and interesting person." That much was true.

The dowager queen pursed her lips and craned her neck to shout, "Elspeth! The boy is lying to my face. Can you believe such cheek?" When no one answered, she turned her stare back to him. "When a man of your age is neither married nor widowed, it tells me that he has no interest in women. Don't bother denying it," she said before he could say anything. "At my age, I have no time or patience for games."

The woman sighed and sipped more of her tea. "So the girl is to go into a passionless marriage. I would have wished better for her." It was almost as if she were simply speaking to herself.

Because he was part of the topic of conversation and the sadness in her voice tugged at him, Aleki tried to ease her mind. "Queen Margrette, I am a man of honor. Whatever I might prefer, I take the giving of my marriage vows seriously, and I will not embarrass her in the eyes of others by seeking pleasure elsewhere. She will have my respect and as many children off me as she wishes. I hope in time, we will form a bond of some affection. What more would you have me do?" His tone was almost plaintive, and it made him cringe inside. He'd thought he had made peace with his fate. *Obviously not. Because I hadn't met Carwyn yet, a reminder of what I want and can never have.* Having the boy there in his home and not being able to act on his desire was going to be unimaginably difficult. But if it eased the princess' mind to have her cousin live with them, it was the least kindness he could show her.

The dowager queen said nothing for a long while, making that line of sweat down his back increase. Finally, she said, "Nothing. This is beyond your control." There was a steeliness in her eyes that had they been facing each other in battle would have made his knees weak. She smiled suddenly. "You are dismissed."

Aleki hesitated only a moment before standing. He bowed and left with steady steps. When the doors to her suite closed behind him, he let his shoulders droop for a second before straightening again and heading back to his apartments. Life was what it was, not what one wished for. By the morrow, he would be husband to Princess Eleanora. They would leave for his home, and he would plot in earnest to find a way to use the Moorcondians who would be following them to crush the Swarm.

* * * *

Carwyn was glad that he'd dressed formally when he'd answered the summons of the dowager queen, because he had no time to change prior to the banquet and speak with Nora before it. He'd already been toying with the idea of speaking with Nora, confessing what had happened between him and the kai when the message had arrived. She was one of only two people he confided in when something bothered him. Cariad was the other, and he was off in literally uncharted waters. But when his troubles involved his cousin herself, it wasn't fair to burden her with them. He'd decided this was the one time in his life when he'd have to keep a secret from everyone and deal with his problems himself. Except now the whole situation had been flipped on its head, and he wasn't sure he still had anything to worry about.

The royal matriarch had used his first audience with her ever to floor him with a suggestion — *no, an order* — that was both brilliant and insane on the face of it. He'd nearly dropped his teacup, and he *had* spilled some on her rug. That mortification was overridden by his astonishment of her plan. He didn't even try to clean up after himself as his mind worked to process what he had heard. The premise of what the queen had laid out for him depended on his being loyal and dutiful to family and country and that he had the guile to pull it all off. Fortunately for him, the dowager queen both knew intuitively what he craved and had given him what was clearly now his heart's desire on a silver platter.

A harried maid opened the door at his tentative knock. "I must speak with Princess Eleanora urgently. It is at the behest of Queen Margrette." That name drop had the desired effect.

He entered the sitting room and could hear the babble of voices that meant Nora was still dressing for supper. Likely her attendants were making more of a fuss over her appearance than she was. Even if this were a happy occasion for her — which this was not — Nora had always been a practical girl who dressed in a more understated way than her cohort. The maid who'd let him in stopped on the threshold of the bedroom and bade him to come with a wave of her hands. He'd been in Nora's bed chamber plenty of times back on the Kenworth estate and had no compunction about entering this female sanctorum. As expected, Nora stood with a long-suffering look on her face as her maids put on the last bit of jewelry and primped her hair.

"Carwyn, such a surprise." Nora's tone was placid but her eyes said "*save me*".

"Forgive the intrusion, your grace. I have a message from the dowager queen. A private one."

With a flick of her hand, Nora sent her ladies scrambling for the door. When they were alone, she frowned. "I had no idea you'd met with her already."

"It was an unexpected invitation, issued this afternoon after Kai Aleki left her suite." He took a deep breath for courage. "Her majesty has issued a command that still has me reeling."

Nora's frown deepened. "Tell me."

"Well…" Unnerved by having to even speak of the crazy plan, he paced in a circle. "She has decided that you and the kai do not suit."

"Huh! I'm sure most people at court have come to that realization. What would she have me do?"

Carwyn stopped in front of her. "You? Nothing — or not much, anyway. It's going to fall on me."

"What is?" Impatience laced her question, and her gaze narrowed in annoyance.

"She wants me to marry Aleki in your place." There, not so hard after all to say it out loud.

Nora said nothing for a few seconds, her eyes wide now. Then, "That is the most ridiculous thing I've ever heard." Throwing up her hands, she began to pace much as he had. "Does she think for one moment that my uncle will try to pull such a switch on the Southern Chain and risk the entire treaty falling apart?"

"She doesn't intend to give him a chance. I'm to go to the ceremony in your place and once it's done, I will be Aleki's wife and you will be free of this arrangement that makes you so unhappy. He and I are better suited anyway, as her majesty wisely pointed out."

"What nonsense. Just because he's a cousin of their prima kailisa and I'm the niece of the king doesn't mean the match is lopsided. Blood is blood."

Carwyn gnawed at his lower lip before answering. "It's not about that. She...um...knows that Aleki prefers the company of...*men*." He wasn't sure why he was being so delicate with her. Nora understood where his interests lay and thought nothing of it.

Nora came to a halt and pressed her fingers to her temples. "Well, that's not surprising, actually. I could tell he was attracted to you."

"Yes, he is, and I am to him. I'm sure we will do well together, physically anyway." There was no point in dragging out the details of the afternoon at this point. He already knew how his body responded to the man's touch. To have that every day would be amazing. "That's why my marrying him makes so much sense." Huffing out a breath, he added, "I think I'm halfway in love with him, too. Silly, I know." Okay, some of what had transpired that day was necessary to voice.

She took his hand. "No, not silly. You've always been a romantic, Carwyn, but I can't ask you to sacrifice the rest of your life on what might turn out to be an infatuation."

"Do you think that's worse than your being married off to someone you don't want at all? Queen Margrette said she didn't want you trapped with a man who doesn't want even the physical part of you. She was adamant that she won't let that happen."

"What Great-Grandmamma wants, she gets, despite who sits on the throne, and she is sweet to worry about me. I suppose she is thinking of her own marriage. Nevertheless, I can't see the king giving in to her about this, not when our very survival is at stake."

"She doesn't intend to tell him anything. It's you she wants to help."

She looked at him with sad eyes. "It's a lovely thought on both your parts, but there is an obvious flaw. I think everyone will notice if you show up instead of me. Without the king's approval—and the kai's—it's not going to happen."

"Ah, that is where the dowager queen's plan is cunning and really scary. She said you have the right to demand a modesty wedding." He hurried to explain before Nora asked the same question he had. "She said that when she was a child, it was still quite the thing. Her own mother had done it. You go to your groom completely covered—an opaque veil that obscures your face and your hair and gloves to hide your hands. I guess the idea was that until she had been officially wed, she was too shy to face the man, even right before the ceremony."

"That's ridiculous."

"For a woman like you, it is. But I can see how it might ease wedding jitters, and it has a romantic quality to it."

Nora pulled away and paced some more. "The idea then is for you to dress as me in private and...but everyone will know it's not me when you speak your vows."

"No vows. It's part of the modesty. The officiant says them for her, and she only has to nod."

"Hmm. It *is* ingenious, except when he lifts the veil at some point after the ceremony, the ploy will be known."

"True. That won't happen until we've retired to our bridal chamber. At that point, though, we'll be married."

"Something that can be annulled easily without the consummation. Do you intend to insist he takes your virginity while you continue to wear the veil? And don't you think he'll notice what hole he fills?"

Carwyn couldn't help blushing at his cousin's frank talk. "I'm rather looking forward to taking care of that little problem."

"I'm sure you are. How about Aleki? He might not be so happy to find his bride comes with some unexpected…body parts."

The rest of Carwyn's skin heated as he remembered the interlude in the garden. "I don't think he'll mind. And once we've lain together, there will be no undoing it. I'll be his wife." The thought of binding himself to the man was both thrilling and terrifying. "Are you in agreement with the plan?"

"It's insane on the face of it," she said, in echo of his own thoughts.

"Absolutely. So are you in?"

Nora didn't hesitate. "Yes."

Chapter Three

Carwyn took a long, hard look at himself in Nora's full-length mirror. It was just the two of them in her bedroom, her having dismissed everyone as soon as he'd shown up. Changing into her bridal clothing had taken a lot longer than he'd expected. He'd never worn girls' clothes before and discovered that they were as fussy in reality as they'd appeared to be. But the layers and the flounces and general frippery served their scheme. His lack of a bosom wasn't obvious, and Nora's small breasts had proved a plus in that regard as well. Harder to disguise was that she was a bit taller than he. Shoes with a heel mostly solved that problem, and the skirt swept the floor, covering up the fact that her dainty wedding slippers had been cast aside. Her gloves fit his similarly small hands, obscuring his more masculine knuckles. Everything that would proclaim him as an imposter was hidden. Everyone would see Princess Eleanora, because that was what they expected. As the dowager queen had pointed out, it was easy to fool people with a sleight of hand. It was what made hucksters so successful. All that was left was to lower the veil to cover his face. With the high neck of the gown, not a scrap of his skin would show.

Nora looked at him from over his shoulder. "This is actually going to work. If I didn't know it was you inside, I would think you were me."

"Your performance last night will ensure it. You even had me convinced that you wanted a modesty wedding."

"Great-Grandmamma helped considerably."

Yes, the dowager queen had made a surprise appearance during supper, and when Nora had stood with her proclamation, the matriarch had quelled the objection written on the king's face. Oddly for his part, Prince Soren acquiesced without a murmur of dissent. That had been perhaps the influence of his wife. Carwyn couldn't help but wonder, however, if the man had some inkling of what was going to happen. *Nonsense, he couldn't possibly know.*

"We'll soon find out if we're going to get away with this." Carwyn lowered the veil himself and blinked to adjust to the suddenly obscured view. *I best not trip over my own feet, or the scheme will be uncovered before I arrive at the altar.*

"I wish I could be there for you."

"Don't you dare try to sneak in, Nora. This will all be for nothing if you are seen."

Nora wrinkled her nose. "I won't. I promise I'll hide away in here until I hear the hue and cry that is bound to occur once you and your...husband leave your bridal suite. That's assuming he doesn't raise the alarm the moment he sees it's you."

Carwyn whirled to face her, enjoying the novelty of the swish of his skirts. "Please don't worry. This will work out. Aleki will accept me. I can be very persuasive when I want to be," he added with a grin that she couldn't see.

He didn't give her any more time to fret or himself a chance to flee from the fear that mounted inside him. *I can do this*. It was a game, that's all—one that held the fate of nations and his own personal happiness. And if he continued to think that way, he would run screaming down the hall. Instead, he picked up the nosegay of delicate green wildflowers and, squaring his shoulders, marched out to the sitting room and to the corridor door. He didn't look back as he left Nora's chambers. The bevy of ladies in waiting made their curtsies and fell in behind him as he sailed as gracefully as he could toward the staircase that would lead him to the royal chapel. He needn't have worried about tripping. The women anticipated the need for help and made sure that his short train and obstructed view didn't cause him to fall. It was something they must do quite a bit for high-born women, given the elaborate gowns. It gave him confidence to make his way to his destination and his destiny.

All along his journey, members of the palace household and the lesser nobles who could not fit into the limited seating greeted him with great courtesies and muted good wishes. They were there to see their princess sacrifice herself for the safety of all Moorcondia. How would they feel once they learned of the ruse? It hardly mattered. He would be gone from here within the day, and no one would dare fault Nora, especially once the dowager queen let it be known that she had hatched the plan, as he was sure she would. As he neared his destination, his heartbeat sped up from excitement as much as nervousness. If all went well, in less than a day, he would be married to a man he desired more than any he'd ever met and would be ushered into the kind of intimacy he'd only dreamed about. *Please, let this work.*

Prince Soren awaited him at the entrance to the chapel. The man was imposing in his full military garb. Then he pinned Carwyn with a narrow gaze that caused his heart to trip—and not in a good way. The moment passed, although it left his heart thumping wildly. The prince stepped up to Carwyn's side and ushered him down the aisle without touching him. That was the beauty of having a modesty wedding. No one, not even family, would lay one finger on the bride until the ceremony was not only over but the marriage also consummated. Carwyn wondered if subterfuge had been the purpose of the custom to begin with. How many times had families substituted the bride for someone else, only to leave the groom trapped once his lust had overtaken his reason?

Then all thought fled as he caught his first sight of Aleki. The kai stood alone, his cousin and only a few of his men hovering to one side, close enough to protect him if necessary. He was dressed in a dark blue, long-sleeved tunic with a high collar and gold embroidery threaded throughout. His kilt was the same color but with no adornment and knee-high dark brown boots met the hem. Those were mere passing thoughts. Aleki's gaze was far too compelling for him to look elsewhere. Carwyn had to work to keep his breath even and his steps steady. This was not *his* man, not yet—not ever, unless he kept his wits about him. When he reached Aleki's side, he kept his eyes cast downward, not that anyone could tell. Staring toward the worn stone floor helped steady him.

King Auden said some words to cement his part of the treaty, then Aleki responded. It was all formal and scripted and of no real concern of Carwyn's. He simply needed the ceremony to start in earnest before he passed out from nerves. The last of Aleki's statement caught his attention, however. How could it not with his ringing tone.

"On behalf of the prima kailisa, I take the treasure that Moorcondia offers in giving me this bride with humble honor and great pleasure." He leaned into Carwyn, only a whisper away from touching him, and spoke so softly no one but he could hear. "You look lovely, Carwyn."

* * * *

Aleki kept up the pretense of the modest bride by not touching Carwyn during the entire wedding breakfast, nor by taking his hand as they walked solemnly to their bridal suite. It struck him as odd that these Moorcondians wedded first thing in the morning and continued feasting and celebrating all day, only to continue to do so with the married couple once they rejoined them for supper, having lain together to seal their vows. His people didn't put such stock in sex being a critical part of marriage, and he could only imagine that virgins of either sex would have a hard time relaxing under such circumstances. He wondered how experienced his wife was in the matter. Carwyn acted bold, but Aleki thought he was probably untried in this one way. He was determined to give the boy the best pleasure possible—afterward they would have a little chat about how Carwyn had come to walk down that aisle pretending to be his cousin.

A few of his men trailed them, but he'd been firm that no one was to enter the chambers unless he explicitly ordered them to. He felt safe enough, and he wanted his wife to be as comfortable as he could be under the circumstances. *My wife.* It was astounding how wonderful those words were to him when he'd dreaded the idea only that morning. Whatever else, he couldn't say he was angry or disappointed in the ploy to provide him with a substitute bride. To the contrary, he was delighted and relieved—and only felt a little guilty about that. Obviously the princess was smarter than he in finding a way out of a marriage she also didn't want. He could only hope Carwyn wasn't upset about his role, his cousin's misery being switched with his own.

As they approached the door to their room, Moorcondian soldiers flanked it and stood at attention. Without being told, Aleki's men took positions beside them. He ushered his wife in with a sweep of his arm and shut them into a large room that was filled with flowers, trays of food, decanters of wine and a large bed covered in white silk. This was a room for seduction, to be sure, and he was glad there was something to eat. Carwyn had only picked at their lavish breakfast, it being difficult no doubt to get food under that silly veil and into his pretty mouth. He told himself that he should go slowly, but his control snapped disturbingly quickly. He took Carwyn by the shoulders and spun him around so that they were face-to-face. The poor boy practically jumped right out of his elaborate gown.

Aleki couldn't help grinning as he lifted the veil to reveal his bride's face. "There he is."

"How did you know?" The question burst passed those luscious lips as Carwyn looked at him with wide eyes. There was curiosity in his gaze, to be sure, but also some trepidation.

He wanted to alleviate any worry that there was going to be some kind of problem. "I'm not displeased. Quite the contrary. And as to how did I know? I don't understand how anyone didn't realize that it was you—or at least *not* the princess."

"Queen Margrette says people see what they want to see."

Understanding dawned. "This was *her* scheme. Of course it was." He chuckled. "Who else would be so bold as to countermand your king? And she saw me for who I am at my core during our short meeting." He rubbed his hands up and down Carwyn's arms in what he hoped was a soothing manner. "I hope she didn't force you into this arrangement." As soon as he said the words, his stomach tightened with worry that Carwyn's answer would hinder what Aleki hoped could be a more fruitful union.

His bride's answer came first in the form of a shy smile. "I didn't require a lot of convincing." The boy lowered his gaze while he licked his lips. "You must know I desire you, and I wanted Nora to be happy." He raised his eyes to look resolutely at Aleki. "Neither of you would have been content married to each other and I... It would have been hard for me to live under your roof knowing that you were beyond my reach." He shrugged. "We all win this way, don't we?"

By way of an answer, Aleki gave into the passion that he'd held at bay. He tugged the veil off Carwyn's head and let it flutter to the floor. Then he untangled the boy's hair from its bun and threaded his fingers through it. This made it easy for him to latch onto his head in order to bring their faces closer, to give his mouth access to his wife. He'd intended to keep this first kiss light and non-threatening, but his pent-up desire had other ideas. Pushing his tongue inside Carwyn's mouth, he swept its every corner while pulling Carwyn's entire body flush against his own. The moment his hard cock had something to press against, a long groan escaped him. He angled Carwyn's head to deepen the kiss and was delighted when the boy embraced him. With the voluminous silk gown between them, it wasn't possible to tell if his bride was also aroused, but the breathy moans he heard was proof enough that his efforts were welcomed.

It didn't take long for the next level of his control to snap. Breaking his mouth away with a little nip on Carwyn's lower lip, he spun the boy around. The fussy line of tiny buttons running from the nape of Carwyn's neck to the top of the bowed bustle made him grunt with frustration. What madness was this to make it harder for a groom to seduce his bride? "Sorry, my dear. If you want, I'll have this repaired." That was all the warning he gave before clasping the gown's collar and rending it in two until it pooled at Carwyn's feet.

The boy squeaked out a little "Oh," yet made no effort to escape Aleki's hold.

For a few moments, he could do nothing except stare at what lay beneath. Carwyn's wardrobe had been completed to the last detail. He wore a lacy chemise of the same white silk and petticoats tied around his slim waist. Here Aleki had an easier time, simply having to tug at the strings to cause the underskirts to likewise fall to the ground. His breath caught at the fetching sight of stockings gartered at the thighs. He would never have imagined that he'd be aroused at the sight of a man dressed as a woman. Carwyn taught him otherwise. *I must have him…now!* Aleki slipped his arms under Carwyn's knees and lifted him up. With a gasp, Carwyn clutched at his shoulders, his cheeks adorably pink and his breathing uneasy.

"Forgive my abruptness, my dear. I simply cannot wait."

"I...I don't want you to." The boy gasped again as Aleki dropped him onto the side of the bed. Carwyn leaned back on his still-gloved hands, his legs dangling. Now his arousal was plain to see, a slender shaft tenting the chemise.

Aleki slipped the heeled slippers from his feet, then took a moment to simply enjoy the sight. "You are exquisite." The hushed, almost reverent tone of his own voice surprised him. Once again, he briefly thought of how he'd nearly dreaded this moment. He would have to think of a suitable gift to send to the dowager queen. There was enough rational thought, however, rattling around inside his head for him to remember who he held in his power. "And innocent of what we are about to do, yes?"

Carwyn's cheeks turned a deeper shade of pink as he nodded. "Yes, but I want it very much. I know you'll take care with me."

The trust was humbling and made Aleki more determined to treat his new wife with the delicacy he deserved. To slow matters down, he began by kissing his way up the inside of Carwyn's leg, from instep to the garter. He kept his gaze on his bride's face as he used his teeth to snag the garter and slide it down. When it came off the foot, he tossed it aside and repeated his efforts on the other leg. Carwyn watched him with his mouth open in a small O, his lips shiny and with a quickened breath. The chance to seduce was a rare one for Aleki. He was finding it much to his liking and took his time rolling the stockings down and off, as well. All that was left now was the chemise and the gloves. Their time would come. For the moment...

Aleki gripped Carwyn's thighs to slide his bottom closer to the edge of the bed. It gave him easy access to what lay under the soft undergarment. Using his head, he nudged the hem up and pressed his face onto the tight balls that greeted him. He took a moment to lave them, enjoying how his efforts caused his bride to gasp and jerk. By the time Aleki moved on to licking up the shaft of the boy's cock, Carwyn was flat on his back, entirely under Aleki's control. *Such trust.* He did not abuse it, nor did he try to tease this first effort at making his bride come. Instead, he sucked the dick all the way in and swallowed hard. Carwyn cried out so loudly that Aleki imagined the entire palace must have heard. And he practically levitated off the bed. Aleki had to work at keeping the boy in place. He smiled around his mouthful and sucked the cock dry.

Aleki eased Carwyn's legs down before plucking at the ribbons of the chemise. It fell away to reveal a smooth chest, pale compared to his own, yet slender and lovely. He couldn't resist tweaking one pink nipple before stripping Carwyn completely. The boy was boneless, allowing Aleki to position him however he wanted. With his head against the pillow, he opened his eyes to slits and watched silently as Aleki took off his own garments. He didn't make a show of it, eager to join his bride in bed, and led with his hard cock.

Carwyn widened his eyes as Aleki knelt beside him. "I figured you'd be big. Do you think it will fit?"

He couldn't help laughing, especially when Carwyn grinned at his own question. "We'll make sure it does." He frowned in the next instant, suddenly realizing that he needed something to ease the way. A woman could be prepared by stimulating her own juices. A man was a different story. A solution occurred to him. "Wait one moment, my dear." Kissing Carwyn briefly, then more deeply when that proved impossible, he dragged himself off the bed and went to the table where the food had been laid out.

He found what he needed and breathed an inner sigh of relief that he didn't have to go ask one of his men to fetch something. It was too soon to let the secret out. The cruet of oil had been intended for the salad, but it was going to be put to a much better use. He waggled it as he went to join his bride once more. "This will help."

Carwyn lowered his gaze, and with a shy smile, lifted his arms up in silent invitation. Aleki swept him into his embrace and began to arouse his bride once more. It didn't take long. Carwyn's cock had already recovered—the benefit of his tender age. Aleki was going to have to work to keep up with the boy, so long as he initiated him into the marriage bed with great pleasure and as little pain as possible. He took his time, coating two fingers with the oil and using them to prepare Carwyn's hole for the invasion. His bride made it easy, opening up to him at the slightest touch and relaxing into the gentle probing. It took nothing at all to make him ready, and while part of Aleki warned him to continue with the preparation, his desire to claim his bride overrode his caution. Besides, Carwyn' eagerness was on clear display. They both wanted this. He positioned himself between the boy's legs and slicked up his own dick before pressing the head of it against the puckered ring that was waiting for him.

Carwyn didn't hesitate to welcome him in when Aleki pushed forward, bending his knees and grabbing hold of his shoulders. He shuddered and stuttered out puffs of breath. Strain showed on his pretty face with his eyes tightly shut now and his two front teeth clamped down on his lower lip. But when Aleki stopped halfway into the boy's ass to give him time to acclimate, his bride used his heels to urge him to move once more. The tightness of that heat greeting him shot pulses of pleasure through his shaft and to his balls. Still, he kept his journey slow, and when he finally bottomed out, he grabbed Carwyn's dick and claimed his mouth.

Carwyn quivered and gasped as his body worked to accept the long, thick cock filling his ass in the most delicious way. He'd dreamed about this moment, imagined it, hoped for it and now that it was truly upon him, all he could think was *this is not what I expected*. No, it was far better. *Amazing*. The discomfort of taking that big dick was nothing compared to the overwhelming waves of pleasure radiating from the places where Aleki thrust into him. And the way Aleki—*my husband*—worked his shaft in rhythm to the fucking, Carwyn came again quickly and even more intensely than when he'd been sucked off. He arched his back as he screamed out his climax, indifferent to who might hear. It was done. Aleki had de-flowered him and now they were truly wed with no one able to pull them apart. Then the sweetest moment of all came. With a masculine roar, Aleki lurched as deep as he could go. Warmth plashed into Carwyn's channel, the perfect end to being claimed.

For a long time, they lay embraced, breathing harshly. When Aleki rolled onto his side and brought Carwyn with him, they stayed entwined and still joined. "Are you all right, my dear?" Aleki punctuated the question with a quick kiss.

Snuggled against the man's broad shoulder, Carwyn nodded. "I can't imagine being better."

"I didn't hurt you?"

"Of course not. You were so gentle. It hurt no more than it had to, and I imagine one gets…looser with experience."

"Indeed." They lay silently for a while longer, Aleki stroking his hand down Carwyn's back. But the man's cock never fully softened and soon it began to swell again, pressing against Carwyn's sensitive tissues. "I fear I want you again, but I don't want…"

Carwyn didn't give his husband a chance to voice his obvious worries. Clamping his hole down on the shaft, he rolled onto his back. Aleki could have stopped him, could have pulled out of him, but he didn't. And this time, as he thrust into Carwyn's ass, he held nothing back.

Chapter Four

Carwyn licked his fingers clean, then put his empty plate aside. It felt positively decadent to be eating in bed, sweetly achy from being thoroughly ravished by his husband, and washed clean from a surprisingly tender sponge bath ministered by the fierce warrior. The man sat cross-legged beside him, watching with his chin resting on his palm as Carwyn devoured the meal he'd brought to him into the bed. The care and tenderness were every bit as wonderful as the sex. Any lingering doubt he might have had over what he'd done melted away in the face of such obvious welcome and approval. Leaning forward, he wrapped his arms around raised knees and stared back at Aleki.

"Thanks for feeding me. I was too nervous to eat anything before the ceremony, and that damn veil made it difficult to do so at the wedding breakfast." He dropped his gaze and grinned. "And I had no idea sex could make one so hungry."

Aleki chuckled. "You are adorable, and I intend to pique your appetite as often as I can."

Carwyn perked up. "I may spend the rest of my days in bed. With you taking care of me, why should I ever leave it?" The answer to that silly question was obvious. Aleki's face tattoos reminded him of the serious problems their union was intended to tackle. Leaning forward, Carwyn traced a fingertip along the pattern bordering one eye. "Did it hurt?"

"Yes." Aleki clasped Carwyn's hand and pressed the inside wrist to his lips. Instead of letting go, he held it against his warm thigh. "That's part of it, taking a small measure of pain to foreshadow that which comes from warfare."

Carwyn didn't like to think of his husband risking his life fighting so he changed tack. "Are tattoos only for warriors?"

"No. Many people get them as part of the passage into adulthood, although usually not on the face."

Carwyn gave as coy a look as he could manage, the food having revived his energy. "Should I get one?"

Aleki's expression told him the man understood the game. He cocked his head. "If you want. Something colorful and in a place only I get to see." That was all the warning he gave before lifting Carwyn and flipping him onto his stomach. He held him down with a grip on his waist. "Right here." Aleki bit one butt cheek lightly, latching his teeth onto the fleshiest part.

"O-oh." Carwyn's breath stuttered in what he knew to be the beginnings of his own arousal. His hole clenched spasmodically in anticipation of what was to come. But want turned to frustration when his husband pulled away and lifted him off the bed to stand beside it. Carwyn tossed his hair out of his face. "Are we going to do it standing up?"

With a laugh, Aleki smacked him on his ass hard enough to make him yelp, more from surprise than the mild sting. "You are incorrigible, my dear. The day grows late, and we are due for supper. All the palace is eager to see the happy couple, I expect."

Carwyn gestured at the two, hard cocks. "I think they're going to see more than expected."

"Indeed. We must practice discipline and get ourselves under control." He walked away, giving Carwyn an excellent view of the man's muscular ass. It was no wonder he could drill Carwyn so effectively.

Aleki opened a wardrobe and pulled out a variety of clothing. He held up a lovely purple silk tunic threaded with gold beads and a matching long kilt. "This is what a bride wears to be married in the Southern Chain. The prima kailisa sent it as a gift for the princess, and while it's feminine, I'm hoping you'll wear it as I present you to the world as my bride." He looked away. "Not that I expect you enjoy wearing women's clothing, but it's just…"

Carwyn couldn't hold back the squeal as he raced over and threw his arms around his husband. "It's a gorgeous outfit, and I'm proud to wear it." He pulled back enough to kiss the man. "It's not so different than what you and your men wear…just prettier." So saying, he took the outfit from Aleki's grasp and held it up to himself. "Perfect."

"Yes, you are." Aleki's voice was soft, and the look in his eyes made Carwyn's knees go weak. "My kailisa," he added before stepping away. "We need to keep our distance. I'm not sure I have the willpower to resist you."

Delighted by knowing he had a strong effect on his man, Carwyn took pity on him as an act of kindness. It was heady stuff to have such sway over someone so powerful. But Aleki was right. They were expected down to supper soon. The thought of facing the king and the rest of the court with the subterfuge caused his stomach to tighten. Then he remembered that Aleki was there to protect him. He would fix whatever needed to be handled. Carwyn didn't have to worry about anything.

The Chainers' mode of dress took little time. Soon he stood in front of the wardrobe's mirror, checking to make sure his outfit was on straight. The soft, gold sandals that accompanied the clothing were a little big but not too much. Best of all, Aleki stood behind him, having readied himself in the blink of an eye. He was braiding a bejeweled thread into Carwyn's hair. It shouldn't have surprised him that his husband was adept at such things, given how he wore his own hair.

When he was done, Aleki stood with his hands on Carwyn's shoulders, staring at them through the mirror. "You are beautiful. I will be proud to present you to your king's court and that of the prima kailisa. There remains only one thing missing," he added with a soft kiss to Carwyn's cheek.

Carwyn watched with keen curiosity as his husband went to get a small box on the table that held the remnants of their meal. He opened it and took something out before returning. The man seemed almost shy, as if that could ever be said of a warrior.

He held up a thin bracelet made of roped gold. "I know your people use rings to symbolize the marriage union, but my people use this. I would have put it on your wrist during the ceremony but for the no-touching rule of your modesty wedding. Will you let me do so now?"

By way of an answer, Carwyn offered his left arm. "Is this the right one?"

Aleki let out a long breath. "Whichever one you want." He clasped the bracelet around Carwyn's wrist and closed it with a small pin attached. Then he raised it to his lips and kissed it. "Now you are mine."

"I was yours the moment I laid eyes on you." The confession spilled out, and Carwyn didn't have time to regret it. His husband's expression told him all he needed to know. "Do I...?" He licked his lips, enjoying how Aleki's gaze tracked the movement. "Is there one for me to give to you?"

Aleki shook his head. "No. A warrior cannot afford to wear jewelry. It can be used against him in battle. But," he added before Carwyn could voice disappointment, "when we arrive back home, I will have a similar band tattooed around my wrist." He held up his right hand. "When I wield my sword, all will see that I am claimed."

"Oh." Carwyn thought he would melt from the romance of it all. But those words *back home* reminded him of how he was leaving his own for a foreign land.

"What is it?" Aleki cupped his face. "Why are you sad?"

"It shows?"

"Your face is like a window into your emotions. Tell me. I would make you happy, my dear."

"It's just...I'm only now truly realizing that my parents and brothers and sister aren't here to share this with me. I won't have a chance to say goodbye to them."

"Oh, my sweet boy." Aleki hugged him, a gesture of purely comfort, not passion. "When this misery of the Swarm is done with, I will bring you back for a visit with them. Does that please you?"

Carwyn nodded, blinking back the tears that threatened to leak out. He was not going to start his marriage by being a sopping ninny. Aleki didn't need that type of distraction. "Yes, thank you. And my brother Cariad is out charting the waters that the Swarm comes from, so perhaps I will see him soon anyway."

"If it is within my power to make that happen, I will do so. He must be very brave, much as you are."

Carwyn laughed. "I wouldn't have said that about either of us. But we were both raised to understand duty."

"I hope marrying me will be more than that for you." Aleki's tone held a hint of worry and perhaps hurt.

"It is!" Grabbing Aleki by his cheeks, he stared into his eyes. "The time we've spent in this room has been the best of my life. I want you, Aleki. Please don't ever think otherwise. When the queen told me of her plan, she may have considered it a command. To me, it was my heart's desire." Carwyn let go, fearing he'd revealed too much too soon. Strong desire was one thing, emotions another.

Aleki said nothing, simply pressed his lips against Carwyn's temple, then held him for a while longer. "If I could stay here with you, I would be the happiest of men. But duty does call, so let us go face the turbulent waters ahead."

The palace guards were well-trained but, to a man, they couldn't hide their surprise when Carwyn walked out of the chamber holding hands with Aleki. The Chainer warriors were better disciplined as they fell into formation behind them. Or perhaps, like their leader, they'd never been fooled to begin with. Carwyn would have shrunk under the open-mouthed scrutiny of all whom they met on their journey back to the dining hall, except that Aleki's hand was like an anchor, keeping him in place and giving him courage that he wouldn't wander off course. No matter how anyone might have treated Carwyn as a lowly family member of the king, they wouldn't dare disrespect him now that he was Aleki's wife. *His kailisa.* He liked the sound of it and he thought nothing of discarding his title of lord. There were lords aplenty in Moorcondia, but there was only one kailisa of Kai Aleki.

The wall of sound coming from inside the dining room fell to a murmur as they were announced by the herald, then cut off into shocked silence when everyone got a look at Aleki's bride. Once again, Aleki's firm grip gave Carwyn courage. He moved through the corridor of space cleared for them with his head held high to approach the dais where the king and his family sat. His every movement was now a reflection of his husband, and he would do him proud. Besides, it wasn't as if the king would have his head lopped off and start the whole thing over again with Nora. *Is it?*

Aleki kept them moving forward, even as King Auden rose, his eyes wide. Aleki brought them to a halt a respectful distance away, and letting go of Carwyn's hand, made his bow. "Your majesty, I present to you my kailisa."

Carwyn didn't have to be told to press his own palms together and do the same. This was the Chainer way, and that was what he now was. He was still grateful when Aleki took his hand again while they waited for the storm to erupt.

The king's expression turned from shock to thunderous. "What the fu—?" He bit back his words when the queen laid a hand on his arm, and after taking a noticeable breath, he turned to Prince Soren. "Where is your *daughter*?"

"I am here, your majesty." Nora stepped forward from the crowd, dressed as a simple lady whom no one would look twice at. She curtsied. "Please forgive the subterfuge, sire," she added before standing quiet and meek, very un-Nora-like.

The king actually sputtered for a few seconds before saying, "You insolent girl. How dare you threaten the treaty and our very existence with this ridiculous prank? Did you know about it?" He tossed the question at Prince Soren.

The man hesitated, much as he'd done before escorting Carwyn down the aisle, and the way the duchess clutched at his arm confirmed that they had both been waiting for this moment to come.

Carwyn didn't want to cause any more strife in the family. "Sire, he did not. And it was my idea." The way Aleki's grip tightened, he knew the man was not happy with his trying to take the blame.

"That's a lie. It was mine. I forced Carwyn to do it." Now Nora was pushing herself more into the open and raised her chin as she stared back at the king.

"Enough!" The voice came from seemingly out of nowhere. Then the crowd parted as the dowager queen came into the room from a side door, flanked by nervous ladies-in-waiting. The old woman was made of iron will but not all that steady. She leaned heavily on a walking stick. "All of this effort to protect one another is misplaced. There is nothing here that requires an explanation or an apology."

The king seemed to deflate as he sat back down heavily. "Of course. Only you would dare such a scheme."

The dowager queen made a mew of disgust. "It is good diplomacy, nothing more. You might have made the decision yourself if you had more imagination. I blame my son for that, may he rest in peace."

"Most revered Grandmamma," the king said through obviously gritted teeth, "I fail to understand why you thought it was best to intervene in this matter." His effort to remain calm was palpable, but no matter who sat on the throne, the dowager queen was no one to trifle with. And this entire family squabble was playing out in front of almost all the court, the room being jammed packed with the highest ranked courtiers and others leaning through doorways. Carwyn couldn't help feeling guilty about that.

"The 'why' is easy. Nora didn't want the kai, and he didn't want her. Carwyn is a member of the royal family and, as such, an acceptable substitution. Plus, it was obvious they would suit each other very well."

The king focused his gaze on where Aleki's and Carwyn's hands were clasped. "I suppose that's demonstrably true, given that our esteemed ally spent the entire day behind closed doors with his male bride."

Aleki inclined his head with a cheery grin. "Indeed, your majesty. Our marriage has been consummated as your law requires, and I'm well-pleased with it."

Not one to embarrass easily, Carwyn still felt his cheeks warm at his husband's praise and the scrutiny of a thousand pairs of eyes. "As am I," he dared to say, although he doubted that the king cared all that much about his feelings. The safety of Moorcondia was what mattered.

The king visibly relaxed, his elbow resting on the arm of his chair. "I am happy for you both, but your pleasure doesn't signify. Will the Southern Chain accept this substitute bride? Is your marriage, and therefore, the treaty binding by your laws?"

Carwyn looked at Aleki, sure that he had the right answer. He wouldn't have married him if it wasn't going to work. Before the man could answer, however, a voice boomed out from the crowd.

"No!"

Aleki considered it a good thing that he couldn't come before the Moorcondian king armed. Otherwise, he would have been sorely tempted to stick a dagger into his cousin's heart. He turned to face Rei as he pushed his way over to him. At the same time, Aleki tried to reassure an obviously distressed Carwyn with a squeeze of his hand. Amazingly, that gesture worked. Carwyn relaxed in his hold and kept his own tongue quiet.

"Cousin, you speak nonsense." Although he kept his tone as even as he could, Rei had to have heard the underlying menace.

Still the idiot didn't back down. After making a perfunctory bow, he focused on King Auden. "Your majesty, I am here to represent the prima kailisa on this diplomatic mission. And as such and on behalf of the Southern Chain, I can assure you that our law recognizes no such thing as a male bride. It's preposterous," he added with a stern nod to Aleki.

Aleki was careful not to bare his teeth. He'd been grateful when his cousin had been sent with him to deal with the tedium of diplomacy and the treaty. Now, not so much. "Your knowledge of our law is surprisingly faulty, given your governmental role, Minister Rei.

There is nothing to prohibit my union with Lord Carwyn."

Always one to think he was the smartest person in the room, Rei still didn't back down. "It is implied. No matter the position of Moorcondia in this matter, our people will not tolerate it."

Aleki suppressed the impulse to give a warrior posture and instead settled on briefly baring his teeth after all with a quick, fierce widening of his eyes as emphasis. He could see his men at the far end of the room, and they had already started crouching. One word from him and they would fight to the death to reach him and his wife. Of that, he had no doubt. But they weren't there to wage war. Diplomacy was the watchword of the day, and if Rei wasn't going to see to it, he would.

"Our people follow the prima kailisa, and she makes the laws. If she approves of my marriage, then so will they." He refocused on King Auden. "As long as Moorcondia is still willing to honor the treaty, the matter is settled."

The king nodded once. "Of course. As your man correctly points out, we are flexible in such things. We've had to be," he added in a mutter. His queen patted his arm, her serene smile a soothing calm in the troubled waters.

Aleki flicked his gaze at Rei. "There is nothing more to say." When Rei opened his mouth, Aleki bit out, "Nothing."

For a moment, Rei's fury flashed in his eyes. The man was smart enough to bank his emotions again. "Yes, my kai." He bowed and stepped away.

The damage had been done, however. Carwyn trembled slightly, not visibly, but Aleki could feel it through their clasped hands. Surprise and some amount of table-pounding had been expected on the Moorcondian side. He had been prepared to deal with that. Rei's objection had blindsided him, an unexpected turbulence. The fool seemed personally offended, which was odd given that like most men, he'd sought pleasure from others during the long voyage, despite being married. It hardly mattered, in any event. Staying through another meal under the strain of the confrontation wouldn't be good for Carwyn. For his sake, Aleki intended to get them out of Moorcondia as quickly as possible.

"King Auden, as much as I and my wife were looking forward to your further hospitality, I believe it would be prudent to leave on this evening's tide. The Swarm isn't resting, and neither should we. With your permission, of course."

No fool he, the king assented. "Certainly. May the gods protect you on your journey."

"Well, that was easier than I expected." The dowager queen's low voice still caught everyone's attention. She tottered over to them and placed a hand covered in paper-thin skin on Carwyn's cheek. "Do us proud and make yourself happy. We may never meet again, but know that I have full faith in you. If I didn't, you wouldn't be standing there in that fetching outfit."

"Yes, ma'am, and thank you."

Dropping her hand, she shot Aleki a look that could turn a man into stone. "Take care of the boy."

"I will." Aleki let go of Carwyn's hand in order to bow to the woman and watched her leave, shooing her ladies away as they tried to help her. "A formidable woman." He turned to bow to the king, then shouted at his men. "Make ready!"

* * * *

Aleki placed a cloak around his wife's shoulders, enjoying tending to him. "My dear, you court sickness standing out here without proper clothing. It is always colder on the open water than it is on land."

Carwyn tugged the covering over his torso but didn't otherwise move from his place against the railing. "Says the man whose chest is bare. I just want to stay until I can't see Moorcondia anymore. It's nearly disappeared over the horizon."

Catching the tears in the boy's voice, Aleki hugged him from behind and was gratified when Carwyn leaned against him. "I'm sorry you are sad."

"Can't be helped," his bride said with a sniff. "I was the same when I left the family estate for the palace. It will pass, because as with then, I'm sure this is a journey I want to make." He turned in Aleki's embrace once all there was left to see was water. "I'm ready to go to your cabin now."

"Our cabin," Aleki gently corrected. "And I'm also keen to retire." With their bodies pressed flush against one another, it was impossible to hide his erection. Happily, Carwyn was in a similar state.

Carwyn rubbed his hard dick against Aleki's thigh. "Me, too. Do you think me shameless the way I want you so much?"

He laughed as he escorted his bride with his arm around his shoulders. "What a delightfully innocent question, my dear. Your enthusiasm pleases me very much."

"Well, your cock pleases me very much, so I guess we're even."

Aleki grunted as if having been punched in the gut. Before he could think better of it, he swept his bride up in his arms and hurried to their cabin. He ignored the knowing grins of his men. Most of them were from his personal guard and unquestionably loyal. Those that had been picked by Rei for the journey were more reserved, yet competent and respectful. They hardly mattered in any event. Right now, his focus was on his wife and making him happy.

He kicked the door shut, then spun Carwyn against it to devour his mouth. *So sweet.* Everything about this boy was desirable and tasty. He wondered if he'd ever get enough of him. Doubtful, and for now, the fire burning inside him made it impossible to be patient. He tugged Carwyn's cloak and kilt off as he continued to plunder his mouth, and because he didn't want to leave that warm, welcoming place, he only rucked up the tunic. The boy's hard cock was waiting for him, but he wanted to stroke as much of the silky-smooth skin of his wife's torso as he could. Such a simple touch shouldn't have aroused him so, yet it did. And he knew from earlier in the day that Carwyn's nipples were sensitive. He pressed them with his thumbs, making the boy moan and writhe.

He broke the kiss simply to give them a chance to breathe easier, although he didn't take his mouth far. Carwyn's smooth cheek and jaw were lovely to nibble at. Leaving the chest, Aleki stroked his palms down his bride's back to squeeze the high, tight ass that he'd claimed, as was his right as a husband. When he slid a finger down the cleft to slip past the puckered ring, he discovered that remnants of the oil he'd used remained. And Carwyn opened for him immediately, pliant and relaxed. He bucked his hips against Aleki, rubbing his dick against his tunic. There was too much between them still, and yet, Aleki doubted he had the patience to stop and undress himself.

"I must have you...*now*," he panted against Carwyn's mouth.

The boy tightened his grip on Aleki's shoulders. "Take me, then. I can't wait—don't want to, don't need to."

He took his bride at his word, confident that the boy knew his own mind and body. It took little to shove his kilt aside to free his dick. Then he lifted one of Carwyn's legs to give access to his hole. Already on board with the plan, the boy jumped to wrap both of his legs around Aleki's waist. It freed him to clasp the sweet ass with both hands and position it just where he wanted. When Aleki pressed his cock against his bride's hole, it opened for him with little effort. He pushed it in, fearful that he hadn't taken the time to prep the delicate body for his invasion yet determined to fill his wife to the hilt. The tight channel gave only enough resistance to sharpen his pleasure, and the long, low moan of his wife told him the enjoyment went both ways. The jerk of Carwyn's dick and the splash of warm cum against his chest banished any lingering worry. Knowing he'd made his wife come was all he needed to lose total control. He pounded into that perfect ass until his own release tore through him moments later.

They leaned against the door, panting and spent, until Aleki found the strength to stagger over to the bed. He managed to tumble them both onto it without his cock slipping free. No surprise there—the damn thing was still hard. He chuckled as he pressed his forehead against his wife's. "You have taken possession of my body. It wants nothing more than to be as close to you as possible."

Carwyn squeezed his hole. "That's only fair, given that you've entirely invaded mine. All the time I stood at the railing, I kept thinking that something was missing. I realized it was your cock filling my ass."

Aleki groaned. "It will be hard to leave you when I have to go to war." He instantly regretted mentioning the reason they were together in the first place.

"Don't speak of it, please. Let's just pretend that we are going to be on this ship forever as a wedding trip."

"I'm sorry. I want to only make you happy and protect you from everything bad."

Carwyn tipped his head back so that they could look at each other. He tugged what was left of Aleki's top knot free and ran his fingers through it. "Such lovely hair," he murmured. "You don't have to worry about me. I'm stronger than I look and can hold my own when necessary. I had to be tough as the baby of the family, trying to keep up with my siblings."

Aleki ran his thumb down one of his bride's cheeks. "You're so young."

"But not a child. I promise you can count on me to be by your side, no matter what, and to watch your back."

The mere thought of Carwyn ever being in danger caused his heart to skip a beat. "A sweet sentiment and one I appreciate. You'll be safe in my home, however, and I will never let the Swarm come anywhere near you."

The sudden fierceness of his emotion caused his cock to pulse and pushing his bride onto his back, he started fucking him again, long and slow this time.

There was no hurry after all. They had many days to enjoy each other before reality intruded.

* * * *

Carwyn sat on the edge of the ship's pilot house, as the sun was making its way past the horizon, trying to stay out of the way of the crew. Aleki didn't permit him to leave the cabin during most of the day because of how brutal the sun was while out at sea, and his fair skin had pinked up the first day of their journey before he'd realized what was happening. That was enough for his husband to fuss and lay down the rules. It was very high-handed of the man, and Carwyn's natural instinct to rebel was quickly doused by his desire to please his husband and to honor the power of a captain on his boat. So, he didn't mind being below decks, but he was mostly bored unless Aleki was with him. The time certainly flew *then*. He didn't think they'd ever tire of fucking—or perhaps they would when they were both as old as the dowager queen. That was if they survived the Swarm. But no, he wouldn't allow his mind to wander there. Besides, Aleki had brought books with him about the Southern Chain, and that was helpful. Carwyn wanted to know as much as possible about his new country before he arrived. And it did chase away a good deal of the tedium of the journey. The one time he'd offered to help with the manning of the ship in any way he could, Aleki's expression made it clear *that* wasn't happening. Like it or not, he was a pampered kailisa.

A crewmember walked by, giving him a quick glare. Carwyn took it in stride. Rei had proven to be a sullen asshole, and his disapproval had rubbed off on some of the men. Carwyn paid it no mind, and he certainly didn't complain to his husband. The last thing Aleki needed was drama on his ship, and Carwyn was a big boy. He could handle a few dirty looks. Fortunately, Rei himself had stayed scarce, not even eating with them at the captain's table. That was fine with Carwyn, and if it bothered Aleki, he made no mention of it. Undoubtedly, Rei had realized that his objection back in King Auden's court had been very poor judgment. Carwyn could only hope that the man's attitude didn't reflect how the rest of the prima kailisa's court would react. Aleki was certain that the woman, herself, would be accepting. Her only concern was with protecting her people, and from what Aleki had said about her, it seemed obvious that she had a soft spot for him.

"Where is your scarf?" Aleki's silent arrival didn't surprise him as it once had. It was as if the man walked without his feet touching the deck.

With a sigh, Carwyn pulled the cloth from out of his long sleeve. "The sun isn't very strong this time of day. I don't need to keep my head covered."

By way of response, his husband merely held out his hand. Carwyn stopped from rolling his eyes and sat dutifully as Aleki wrapped the scarf around his head, tying it at the back. "I will take no chances with your health." The highhandedness melted away with a sideways hug that drew Carwyn tightly against him.

They sat quietly for a while, simply enjoying the time together. It wasn't sex, but just being with each other for any reason was satisfying, and knowing that, Carwyn's burgeoning love for his husband gained strength. He still kept those thoughts to himself. It was too soon to voice strong emotion to a stoic warrior who might never love him back. It was enough for now and perhaps forever that the man wanted him with an obvious intensity.

A dot in the distance caught his eye. "What is that, an island"?

"Yes, one of hundreds if not thousands in these waters. We'll pass by many of them from now on. It's likely uninhabited by people, as most of those that I've stepped on have been untouched by humans, although the larger ones usually have sources of fresh water, small game and edible flora."

"That's good, about there not being people on them. One less place tempting for the Swarm to ravage."

"But also one that they can easily establish as a base as they make their way to Moorcondia and other places. It will help them resupply their ships, so they don't have to risk raiding more often than they want to. It's what I would do as a strategy. I have to assume they are as clever as they are vicious."

"Oh." He laid his head against his husband's chest. "You won't let that happen, though."

Aleki kissed the top of his head. "I was committed to that before I left for your country. Now, I have even more of a reason to stop them. And with the Moorcondian ships joining us soon, we'll give the Swarm something to reckon with."

The man sounded so sure. Carwyn let himself trust in that and enjoyed the setting of the sun.

Chapter Five

Something roused Carwyn from his deep slumber. He sat up, clutching at the bedsheet and straining to make out the noise filtering into the cabin. It was bad, that much was clear. Muted cries and running feet sounded the alarm that there was a problem—a big one. Aleki was already out of bed, his movements barely visible by the moonlight streaming through the porthole. The speed in which he first wrapped a kilt around his waist, tied his top knot, then pulled a sword out of a trunk confirmed that there was trouble. "What's happening?"

A pounding on the door caused Carwyn to jerk. "My kai, we are under attack. The Swarm has found us." Rei's voice was easy to discern yet held none of the haughty contempt he was prone to use, even with Aleki.

When Carwyn started to get out of bed, his husband stopped him with a curt order. "Stay there." He opened the door. "Status?" he barked out to a barely visible Rei.

"They've boarded and we've already taken losses. We need you, my kai."

"How did they get past our sentries?"

"I don't know but right now, we are fighting for our lives."

"I'm coming." Aleki shut the door in his cousin's face and strode over to the bed. He all but lifted Carwyn off using one hand and set him on his feet. "Did you bring a knife with your belongings?"

Carwyn tried not to show how scared he was. "Of course. Just about everybody in Moorcondia carries a knife for personal protection."

"Good. Get it and keep it close." Tugging Carwyn toward the door, he added, "Bolt this behind me and don't open it up, no matter what, unless I tell you to. Understand?"

"Y-yes."

Aleki hauled him up to his toes for a quick, hard kiss, then peeking around the door, slipped out and shut it again. Carwyn hesitated only a moment before doing as told and sliding the two large iron bolts, one on the top and one on the bottom, into place. Then he leaned against it with his heart pounding and mounting fear that threatened to swamp him. The sounds of the battle were clearer now, and his heart wrenched at the thought that his husband was out there in the thick of it. Knowing that he would do no good if he collapsed into terror, he hurried to the bed and pulled his trunk out from under it. The dagger he'd been given by his father was in its sheath and tucked beneath his clothing. He didn't hesitate to pull it out and strap it to his thigh before shoving the trunk back into place.

Carwyn sat on the edge of the bed, listening and worrying before realizing that while he meant to be a biddable wife to Aleki, he wasn't a helpless ninny. He knew how to use the weapon he wore — of course he did, having been schooled in fighting. And he wasn't half-bad at soldiering, merely indifferent. There was no question the situation they were in was dire, and one man could make a difference in the winning or losing of the fight. Besides, he couldn't bear the idea of sitting in hiding while his husband was possibly losing his life. What would be his fate in that event? The door wouldn't hold the Swarm for long, and they probably wouldn't grant him a quick death. The rumors of enslavement made his blood freeze, a hideous fate. And he might be passed around by them until he died from the abuse. Better to go down with a blade in his hand.

Having made up his mind, he wrapped his kilt around his waist and caught up his hair in the scarf. Leaving it down might give an opponent something to grab on to and take him down. Thinking of it made him appreciate why Aleki and his warriors wore theirs up. And now it was time for him to join them. He placed an ear to the door to listen for any fighting in the corridor and hearing nothing close, dared to unbolt and open it. The moment he did, the battle sounds were louder. He cringed and nearly retreated to the relative safety of the cabin. But his husband was out there, and he needed to be by his side. He slipped out and cautiously made his way to the deck.

At the bottom of the stairs, Carwyn could now see the pitched battle being waged. He watched for a chance to join them without interfering with any engagement by Aleki or his men. They didn't need him as a distraction that might prove fatal. He had to believe that they were seasoned warriors and his addition to the fray could lead to more problems than help. And yet, he was determined to try, so he watched the dancing of mostly bare feet past the opening and took the chance to go up. Even as he did so, a part of his brain registered that something was off. He didn't realize what until he got a good look at the scene playing out on deck. Instead of getting his first look at the vicious Swarm, all he saw were Chainers...fighting each other. Shock caused him to falter, and as he looked on with horror, Aleki and many of his men were forming a tight circle. They were surrounded by even more of the crew, however. The numbers were not in their favor.

"Ha!" A beefy warrior with blood streaking his chest grabbed Carwyn's arm and hauled him up the last step of the passageway.

All those tedious lessons with his family's master arms trainer kicked in. Carwyn lashed out to kick the side of the warrior's knee while wrenching his arm free. He ran without thought past the ring of aggressors and to Aleki's left side.

His husband let out a whoosh of breath. "My dear, I really wish you had stayed in the cabin as ordered."

He tried not to crowd the man, even as the advancing warriors turned his guts to water. "Remaining trapped in there didn't seem like a good idea." The press of his sheath against his thigh made his fingers itchy to grab it. With the ever-tightening circle of defense, he was afraid he'd stick his husband with it by mistake.

"I find it hard to argue with your logic. Still, when this is over, I will school you on the difference between a husband and a captain. Obeying orders is critical to run a ship. Otherwise, you end up with…"

"This," Carwyn finished. He was trying to remain calm, or at least giving the appearance of being so, like Aleki was doing. Their opponents kept up their warrior grimaces and grunting, yet made no further attempt to attack.

The reason why was revealed when Rei strode through the line. The fucker was smiling and had not a scratch or spot of blood on him. "Ah, cousin, we seem to have you surrounded."

"You were always one to state the obvious," Aleki replied in a dismissive tone.

Rei curled his lip. "I would watch your tongue, Aleki, or I'll cut it out and feed it to the fish."

"I expect that's my fate anyway." It was amazing how steady the man's voice was, even in the face of death.

"On the contrary, I want you very much alive. The Swarm are eager to sacrifice you to their god of blood. The prima kailisa's chief warrior will be a worthy one, to be sure, and the Swarm do put a lot of store in their ceremonies."

Now Aleki did show emotion. "You're in league with them!"

"As all intelligent people are. They cannot be stopped, so why not join them? It was an easy decision to come to, although approaching them was not without risk to my own neck. That I did so is proof I am the right person to rule the Southern Chain. The Swarm are vile, but they are also cunning. Allies are beneficial to them."

"You dare to aspire to the throne? There are plenty in our family that stand between you and it. Will you kill them all? Are you that mad to think you can get away with it?"

Rei scoffed. "*Warriors.* You are so simple, thinking everything can be solved with a sword. And to be fair, some can be." He gestured to his cadre of men. "But my plans are more subtle. The prima kailisa will have to meet an untimely end. The rest...?" He shrugged. "I know how to maneuver around the court to get what I want."

"You are a consummate politician." The way Aleki said them, the words were not a compliment. "But you have shown your hand too soon. The Moorcondian fleet heading this way expect my wife to greet them." There was a quiver of emotion now in his voice, and he moved close enough to bump Carwyn's hip with his own. "They will want answers when he doesn't, and they are not fools."

Rei flashed a look of hatred at Carwyn. "The plan was flawless. The princess was supposed to remain in your cabin until I, her cousin by marriage, came to liberate her with the sorry tale of your brave death before I was able to heroically defeat the attacking Swarm. Below decks she would have never known what truly happened, and I could keep her down there until I'd passed you and what was left of your men off to the Swarm ship that's on its way for our rendezvous."

"You truly believe the Moorcondians would settle for a dead husband and widow to keep the treaty?"

"Certainly not. I would have taken her as my second wife, as is my right, and my current one knows her place well enough to make no fuss about it. As the captain, I have the power to marry anyone, even myself, while at sea. And as her new husband, I could keep the princess safe. Family honor demands no less, and a frightened woman welcomes the protection of a man. Instead, you married this ridiculous excuse for a wife, and he didn't stay put. A girl wouldn't have come on deck in the middle of a fight."

"You don't know Nora very well," Carwyn couldn't help saying.

"Hush," Aleki admonished in a low tone. "Your plan has been thwarted. There is no princess for you to exploit. What now? We will not surrender to you." To emphasize his point, Aleki raised his sword higher.

"Won't you?" Rei took a step forward. "You're the prize the Swarm wants. My men have orders not to kill you. The others...?" He shook his head. "Even your slut has no great use for me. He's very pretty, and I might have been able to enjoy dragging him to my bed, but I can't trust him, given what he knows. I think the Swarm would pay a great deal for him, given his novel looks, but I must see to the greater good and think of a new plan." He signaled with his hand and a warrior armed with a bow and arrow stepped up and aimed his weapon at Carwyn.

"The choice is simple, Aleki. Surrender and you, your *wife* and what's left of you men live. You won't for long once I hand you over to the Swarm. The others will be enslaved. Not a pleasant life — but still, a life. I know your optimism, cousin. Live to fight another day. That's what you're thinking now, even though you're wrong about that."

Long seconds ticked by before Aleki slowly lowered his sword. "I'm sorry," he whispered before dropping it. He pulled Carwyn into his embrace as Rei's warriors overpowered them.

* * * *

Carwyn snuggled against Aleki in the filthy straw littering the hold. "Are you very mad at me?"

"Very. I'm lying here considering all the ways you should be punished." In direct contradiction to his words, Aleki pulled his wife in closer and kissed the top of his head. Fear of what awaited the boy once he was in the hands of the Swarm threatened to swamp in. He mustn't let it. Their only hope of escape required a clear head, not one clouded with emotions.

Carwyn patted his chest as if to give comfort. "I won't mind, as long as you get a chance to mete it out."

"We will. I won't let that bastard sell you off to the Swarm." He wanted to call out to his men, who were imprisoned in the other cages they'd put in the hold specifically to take members of the Swarm captive. It had never occurred to him that he'd end up here himself. At least he and Carwyn had their own space while the others were crowded in together. Rank did have its privileges, and right now, he was grateful for it. Carwyn must be disgusted and petrified in equal measure. And yet, the thought of the boy having remained in the cabin and becoming Rei's wife and pawn wasn't much of a better predicament.

"Being their slave sounds horrid but not as bad as what they intend for you. Do they really practice blood sacrifice? I thought that was a rumor."

"Apparently it is not. Don't worry. I won't let that happen, either." Bold words, considering he had yet to work out a plan.

There was no way to know for sure how long they had before they reached whatever rendezvous spot where Rei had agreed to meet the Swarm ship. A few days more of sailing, perhaps. They had to break free somehow. The cages were padlocked, and there was nothing to use to open them. Only one guard was down there, obviously bored and drinking from a flask. His sleepy-eyed face was lit by the dim light of a lantern, yet even if he could be somehow overpowered before alerting the others, he didn't seem to have any keys with him. *Rei is too cautious for that.* The mere thought of his cousin had him clenching his fist as he imagined he held the man's neck.

Carwyn derailed his thoughts by pressing his mouth against his ear. "Do you trust me?"

When Aleki nodded, his bride took his hand and slid it down his thigh. The feel of the sheath and the hilt of the dagger within it caused Aleki's heart to skip a beat. Here was hope, and what a clever boy his wife was and how dumb of Rei not to think to search him for weapons. In fairness, however, he hadn't expected his wife to be armed, either, assuming he'd not followed orders in that regard, when he didn't see the weapon in his hand.

Aleki started to ruck up Carwyn's kilt, but the boy stopped him. "I have an idea. Please…follow my lead." He waited until Aleki once again nodded before smacking his chest and pushing away. "Get your hands off me!" Carwyn skittered away until his back hit the bars of their cage. "You disgust me. Do you think I'm going to let you fuck me here in this filth with your men watching and listening? Why, because you know once the Swarm has us, your life is forfeit and you want to use me while you can? This is all your fault!"

Being a warrior meant being quick and flexible, adapting to any change in the situation. He'd done it already when he'd realized it was Carwyn and not

Nora under that veil. This time was no different. His wife was putting on a performance, and he had a role to play as well. Aleki raised himself to a crouching position. "Get back here. You're my wife and will do as you're told. If you'd obeyed me earlier, you wouldn't be lying here. So stop your whining and come back here before I drag you by your hair."

Carwyn shook his head violently. "No. If I'm going to be a fuck toy for other men, I should at least start now and have a clean place to lie and some water to wash with." He banged on the cage bars. "Warrior, come help me, please!"

The guard, like everyone else in the hold, was watching the fight play out. "Shut up." He took a slug from his flask.

Carwyn stuck one hand out beyond the bars. "Please, sir. I'm sorry I don't know your name, but if you let me out, I'll show you my gratitude." The boy gave a watery smile. "I don't want to stay in this horrid place and will do anything to earn my freedom."

The guard gulped down more drink before putting the flask aside and coming slowly toward their cage. The look in the fucker's eyes caused murderous rage in Aleki, yet he knew that whatever Carwyn was going to do, he had to let it play out. "Stay away from him. Don't you dare touch him." To make his threat real — or more real, because he sincerely didn't want the asshole touching his wife — Aleki started to rise as much as the cage permitted.

The guard drew his sword and stuck the tip between two bars. "If you want to keep your skin, kai, stay back." He flicked his gaze down Carwyn. "You think I'm a fool, slut? Prove yourself useful." He flicked his kilt aside, freeing his stiff cock. "Make it good, and maybe I'll let you out."

The growl that pushed past Aleki's lips was not feigned. He worried that his wife would have to take the ruse farther than either of them could tolerate. It was still the best way for them to free themselves, although he had only an inkling of what the boy would do, and the thought of that sword piercing his heart before he succeeded caused his lungs to freeze.

Carwyn straightened on his knees and brought his mouth closer to the bars. "I'll make it good. You'll see."

The guard stuck his vile dick through the bars. As Carwyn leaned into it, there was only the sounds of harsh breathing, every man there watching. Aleki knew his men thought the worst of his wife at the moment. None dared say anything, though, and he didn't want to risk signaling them with even a look. The guard's focus fixed on the sight of Carwyn's open mouth heading for his cock. There was no chance he'd see how the boy reached under his own kilt and drew out the dagger. Rei's man gasped with his mouth open like a gutted fish as Carwyn plunged the weapon right under this cock. Knowing it wouldn't be enough to kill him quickly, Aleki sprang from his spot. He pushed his wife to the side as he grabbed the dagger with one hand and the guard's leg with the other. He swept him off his feet and down to the floor before piercing him through the heart.

Aleki gave himself a moment to catch his breath, before swinging toward his wife and pulling him by his hair into a hard kiss. "You are brilliant, my dear, but I'm still angry at you. Now to free us all," he added, shooting his men a grin.

The dagger proved to be only marginally useful at picking the padlock. It was better than what they'd had before, which was nothing. Still, he had to work the mechanism for far too long. As time ticked by, he concentrated on his task and counted on his men to keep a look out. Sooner or later, the next warrior on watch would come down and their chance at escape gone. Finally, the lock clicked, and he was able to free himself and his wife. There were three more to go, however, and he worried there wasn't going to be enough time. And there was only the one sword available, hardly sufficient to retake the ship. Before he could start on the next cage, footsteps caught his attention. Pushing Carwyn back into their cage, he shut the door, then went to stand by the entrance. The replacement guard didn't have a chance. Aleki had his hand over the man's mouth and the blade across his throat before he took one step into the hold.

"So much blood." Carwyn came to join him, his gaze fixed on the dead man. He wiped his hands repeatedly down his thighs. It was then that Aleki had time to consider that his wife had tried to kill a short while ago and probably for the first time.

He pulled him into an embrace. "Don't look at them. Don't think about it. You have freed us, and now we have a chance that we didn't before."

Carwyn nodded and stepped back, giving him space to work on the other locks, except his right-hand man, Lono, stopped him as he stepped to the nearest cage. "My kai, there is no time. Save yourself and the kailisa. Our fate is sealed for now, regardless, but with you out there, we have hope of being rescued."

Aleki looked into the faces of all his men and saw they were in agreement with Lono—and the man was good at battle strategy. He made hard calls, and Aleki could do no less. "I will come for you, even if I have to sail straight into the mouth of the Swarm." He gathered the fallen guards' swords and relieved them of the knives sheathed at their thighs. He stuck one sword and one knife into the tie of his kilt, handed Carwyn back his dagger, and silently crept up the stairs with the second sword at the ready. Carwyn didn't need to be told to follow him. The boy was being as quiet as he could, yet every time the stairs creaked under his footstep, Aleki stopped to listen if anyone approached. As they reached the deck, he scanned the area. Dawn was only just starting to show at the horizon. What crew was about did their work lazily, not expecting anything much to happen before the day began. They were also drinking, and the few words that drifted his way told him they were entirely too smug in what they'd done.

Aleki crept toward the stern, Carwyn sticking to his shadow. When they reached their destination, he had a decision to make. He was relieved to see that the chain of uninhabited islands was still close by. If they could make it to one of them, they had a chance of evasion and a defensible position. But if they used one of the lifeboats for the journey, it would make too much noise. They'd be discovered quickly and retaken before they could make their escape. The only other choice was not much better.

He leaned to speak into Carwyn's ear. "Can you swim?" When the boy nodded with obvious confidence, Aleki's hopes rose again. He motioned his wife forward. Then grabbing one of the ropes they used to inspect the hull, he slowly fed it down to the water. There was no way he was going to make it to the island carrying swords, so he reluctantly set them aside and shoved the second knife into his waistband. Then he crouched and beckoned his wife to get onto his back.

Instead, Carwyn whispered into his ear. "I can climb, too." He rolled his eyes when Aleki glanced back at him.

Fair enough. He'd have to trust that his wife knew his own limitations, and hadn't the boy proved himself to be surprisingly capable? Making no more effort to communicate, he helped Carwyn over the side of the ship and watched him start his climb down. There was nothing to fear, his bride showing great agility and speed. Aleki needed to hurry to catch up to him. With one last look at his ship and a silent vow that he would return, he made his way to the sea. It was shockingly cold after the heat of the hold. Carwyn waited for him, treading water and showing admirable courage. The distance to any of the islands was farther than he would have liked but needs must. He pushed off from the side of the boat and headed for the safest place, his bride by his side. Carwyn had been truthful about his ability to swim, but the distance would be great. They might drown before they reached land. *No, I will not let that happen.* If it came to it, he would drag his wife to safety, fear for the boy making him determined and giving him strength.

Chapter Six

Aleki helped his wife climb out of the ocean and over the rocky shore. He didn't stop until they'd reached the relative cover of a stand of trees. There had been softer places to enter the island, but sand left footprints, and he wanted to avoid that. Rei's warriors would be good at spotting the signs, no matter what he did to obscure them. As skilled as he was at such warfare matters, he wasn't going to take any more risks with Carwyn's life than necessary. They both dropped like stones, the arduous swim having taken every ounce of energy either of them had. Panting on their backs while staring up at the sky with its rising sun was all that was possible. He'd never been so exhausted and had only enough strength to move his hand in search of Carwyn's. He held it for the comfort that it brought him and hopefully the boy. It was amazing they'd made it to landfall at all, and Carwyn hadn't needed any help. The boy was a marvel and had even managed to keep the scarf on his head to protect him from the sun that would soon beat down on them.

But there was not much time for rest. He allowed them to sleep for a short while before rousing them both. Soon, their escape would be noticed, if it hadn't been already. The next phase of their on-the-fly plan had to start. And happily, Aleki saw they were in luck. He reluctantly let go of Carwyn's hand and went to the nearest tree. Climbing was easy for him, always had been, even though his arms screamed from the effort. He ignored the pain as he'd been trained to do and focused on the prize waiting for him. Lily fruit hung from the tree. The sight of it gave him a boost in confidence that his decision to head for this particular island hadn't been a fatal one. The fruit would provide sufficient liquid, even if they found no fresh water source and the meat as well as the seafood surrounding them would sustain them for a long time. But he wasn't interested in simple survival. He had to be prepared to fight Rei's men when they followed them — and they would — and figure out a way to return to the ship and take it back.

"Watch out below." Using one of his knives, he hacked four of the fruit pods off their vines to tumble down to the ground. By the time he joined them, Carwyn had managed to sit up.

He held one in his hand. "How do we open them?"

Aleki grinned as he took it and used his knife to slice it in two. The juice ran down his arm. He licked it up before handing half to his wife, who scrutinized the offering with an adorable expression. "Like this, my dear." He demonstrated how to eat it by sinking his teeth into the flesh and scraping it away from the rind. His mother would have been appalled at his table manners, but they weren't at a banquet — and damn, it tasted fantastic.

Carwyn copied him and moaned. "So good! I'm parched after that long swim in water we couldn't even drink. I'm used to lakes and rivers," he added, taking another bite.

The juice dribbled down his wife's chin, a delectable temptation. He wanted to lick it up. Before he could follow through on the impulse, Carwyn wiped at it with the back of his hand. The look he shot Aleki told him he knew what was on his husband's mind.

They ate two of the lily fruits in quick order before resting again. "I'm sorry we won't be able to sit here for much longer. We need to move farther into the island and find the most defensible position." He cast his gaze out to sea. The ship wasn't visible yet. "It won't be long before they sail back to look for us. Hopefully Rei will send his men to the larger, closer island first. It gives us time to fortify ourselves."

"That's why you had us swim farther to this smaller island." Carwyn brushed at his skin as he spoke. "I hate how the salt water is drying on me."

"There may be a source of fresh water that you can bath in."

"That would be nice. I understand, though, that survival comes before comfort." The boy dropped his gaze. "Um, you did know what I was doing back there, right? I mean, you understand it was all a ruse to get the guard within striking distance?"

"My dear wife…" Aleki scooted closer and took Carwyn's face in his hands. "Of course, I did. How very clever of you to secret that knife under your kilt and woo the guard to his death." He kissed him gently. "Rei underestimated you…as did I."

Carwyn threw himself into his embrace. "I was so scared. And when I stuck the knife in, it was so disgusting—squishy and wet—and I swear I can still smell the blood."

Aleki hugged him tight, wishing he could take the horror of it onto himself. "Hush now, darling. I'm sorry for it. You should never have had to fight for your life...or mine. I wish I could promise I'll shield you from more of it. I can't. We must take a stand here, and more blood will be shed before it's done."

"It's okay. I understand, and if it means saving you and our people, I can do whatever is needed. My father made sure I had lessons in how to fight," he added with a sniff. "I'm not afraid, so long as you're by my side."

Such simple trust. Aleki hoped he would live up to it.

* * * *

Carwyn tried to concentrate on whittling his sticks to sharp points so that he didn't scrape off any of his own skin in the process. It was hard not to scan the area for movement or strain his ears to pick up anyone landing on the island. He felt as if any moment, they'd be set upon by the traitorous Rei and his minions, but Aleki was confident that they had more time to fashion their weapons and set their traps. It took a while to turn a ship around, given the dependency on the direction and force of the wind, and with other choices for where they might have escaped to, he didn't expect this would be the first place they'd look. Carwyn wasn't convinced, yet he trusted his husband to have better judgment than he about war strategy. And that was what this was—a civil one, but warfare, nevertheless. How many other Chainers were in on this with Rei? They'd have to be rooted out before the Moorcondian fleet arrived to avoid further sabotage. There could be many of them at all levels of power, ready to wreak havoc without warning. Worrying about the open aggression of the Swarm seemed easy in comparison.

He held up his stick. "Is this sharp enough?"

Aleki looked over from where he was sharpening far bigger branches. "It will do, yes. We'll need as many more of those arrows as you can manage. I'll make the bow once I'm done with these."

Carwyn wrinkled his nose as he eyed the lethal-looking weapons. "Those aren't for archery, are they?"

Aleki didn't laugh at his obviously silly question. With a sigh, he said, "No. This is for a trap, a horrible one in which no one who falls in it will come out again alive." He closed his eyes for a moment. "I hate this. I hate having to expose you to the ugliness of men killing each other."

"I'm not so fragile. I've studied plenty of battles and understand how brutal they are."

"Words and pictures. They're not the same as seeing it with your own eyes — smelling it, having gore cover your hands and splatter on your body." He swore. "And I'm not helping with this kind of talk. I swear I won't let any of them touch you." The look in his eyes was fierce. More, there was a hint of fear, and Carwyn knew it was for him, not Aleki himself.

"I don't need reassurance on that front." He tossed his head and picked up another branch. Time to change the subject — sort of. "What was all that about Rei taking a second wife? Is that a thing in the Southern Chain?"

"Technically, yes. There is no law prohibiting someone from taking as many spouses as they wish. It's mostly the older generation that still practices it, if for no other reason than the prima kailisa has decreed that you can't take another spouse unless the existing one or ones agrees to it. As he said, Rei's wife would go along with whatever he wanted."

"But polygamy isn't permitted under Moorcondian law." He hadn't considered it was an issue at all. Now he did for no other reason than he'd assumed he wouldn't have to share his husband with anyone.

Aleki scrutinized his stake before starting the next one. "Which is why I was sent to seal the treaty. Plenty of others would have been closer to the throne and therefore more worthy — except Nora would have been a second wife, and that wouldn't have been acceptable to your king."

"That's certainly true. Why do you suppose Rei thought he could get away with it?"

"I don't think I'm a good judge of what goes on in that man's mind — not under the circumstances. His treachery was a complete surprise, and that lack of discernment bothers me. Perhaps his poor wife was next on the list to have an 'accident'."

"You can't blame yourself." Carwyn wanted to give the man a hug, but they didn't have time, and Aleki probably didn't want such reassurance. He was too much a leader and proud with it.

Aleki paused his work and leaned over to stare at him. "I am the captain of my ship and the chief warrior for my people. The fault lies with me, no matter what. I could lose my position over this once I drag Rei in front of the prima kailisa for punishment. You may find yourself wedded to an ordinary warrior or even one retired in ignominy."

Carwyn huffed. "As if I care about such things as status. I don't like your being scapegoated for this. You are the best person to lead the Chainers against the Swarm."

His husband said nothing in response for a long while, opting to return to his task. "I don't know what I did to earn your trust like that. All I am is the man you were forced to marry and who has failed to keep you safe." He flicked his gaze back at Carwyn. "You humble me, wife."

"Don't be stupid!" Dropping his half-finished arrow, he looked away, blinking back sudden tears. "No one *forced* me to do anything and if you were a lowly soldier in my king's army, I would have still wanted you. You can't know how much," he added in a low voice. Then he clamped his lips shut before he let his true feelings blurt out. Aleki didn't need the drama of a weepy wife professing love.

Strong arms encircled him in a tight hug before he realized Aleki had moved. "Don't cry."

"I'm not." The denial was undermined by his watery voice. He wrapped his arms around his husband and held on as if he could never let go.

"I promise I will protect you now. We'll overcome any attack and return to take back the ship." Aleki punctuated his promise with a kiss on Carwyn's head before gently separating them. He clasped Carwyn's wrist and rubbed a thumb along the marriage bracelet he'd given him. "It gives me heart to see this survived our journey."

"Me as well. It's proof our bond is strong. Not even the ocean can break it." He immediately felt foolish at voicing the sentiment. No doubt Aleki didn't ascribe to such romantic notions. He was wrong.

His husband placed a kiss to the metal before letting go. "I like to think so. Now, we must hurry to finish everything before nightfall."

Carwyn didn't hesitate. He picked up his stick and rededicated himself to making as many arrows as he could. In this way, at least, he would be an asset to his husband.

* * * *

Carwyn spread his kilt and scarf out on the rocks with the hope that the setting sun would prove strong enough to dry the cloth. They'd been lucky, finding a decent spring of fresh water and being able to sluice off the worst of the sea salt residue from his skin, hair and clothing. He felt nearly normal again, if one counted being naked on a deserted island, waiting to be attacked as *normal*. The not-wearing-clothes part was kind of fun, especially as it gave Carwyn an excellent view of his husband's strong physique. He hoped the man was equally enticed by his own nakedness, although it was probably a bad idea to distract themselves with sex when they could be set upon at any moment. The outcrop of rocks where they were making their stand was sufficiently tall for Aleki to spot the ship offshore. The sandy beach in the line of sight was the best place for a boat to land, at least as far as they could see. The island was big enough that there hadn't been time to scope it out entirely. Aleki had decided this was the most likely location and that battle-honed judgment was something that Carwyn relied on without question. And they would be pursued, that was a certainty. Even though Rei couldn't afford to send out multiple search parties, those that were searching for them would eventually make their way to this location.

We're ready for them.

He made himself feel confident because Aleki exuded it, and maybe the man was merely doing it to calm Carwyn, but that was fine. He was willing to be comforted, even if their odds of succeeding were low. He chose to believe Aleki and the wicked weapons and traps they'd set certainly appeared up for the job—so long as Rei's men acted and reacted the way Aleki anticipated. And that was another thing he had to assume his husband was right about. These were men trained as he was—and even by him at some point. Predicting their next moves was more than guesswork.

As he stood watching his husband, he allowed himself to enjoy the view and forget about the rest. Worrying never solved anything. And when Aleki turned toward him, all wet from his dunk in the water, he telegraphed that he'd been thinking about Carwyn. His thoughts were evident by his hard cock jutting out from his pelvis. His large balls were tucked tightly against his body, a function of both arousal and the increasing coolness of the night. Simply seeing it was enough to cause Carwyn to have the same reaction.

He gave his man a shy smile as he approached. "I feel better, don't you?"

Aleki cocked an eyebrow while setting his kilt near Carwyn's to dry. "We were lucky to have access to so much fresh water." He flicked his gaze at Carwyn's crotch. "And I can see we are both refreshed considerably. Sadly, we must ignore that hunger and feed our stomachs instead." Taking Carwyn's hand, he walked up to the top of the rock formation to where he'd stored food. The man had actually taken the time to make a nice little nest of the area. "Sit. I'll serve you."

"You don't have to do that."

"I like pampering you." With a glance around, he added, "There's little opportunity to do so in our current situation."

Carwyn didn't want his husband's guilt to grow, so he sat on a reasonably flat stone with no further fuss. The seat was cool on his ass and a little rough, but those were minor discomforts. When Aleki handed over a freshly cut half of a lily fruit, he bit into it with gusto. They'd worked hard and with little chance to eat more after their first meal. "Hmm. This is delightful."

"Not filling, though, or filled with the kind of nutrients we need." He picked up one of the mollusks he'd gathered from the rocky shore before they'd made their camp and deftly opened it with his knife. "These will give us energy—and they are tasty, too," he said, holding one half in front of Carwyn.

He didn't want to be ungrateful, and he knew fruit alone wasn't going to be a good meal, but the thing lying inside the shell looked rather like snot. "You eat them raw?"

"It's too dangerous for us to risk a fire. The smoke would carry above the trees and lead our enemies right to us. Many people choose to eat them uncooked, anyway. The flavor is purer that way. And you don't chew, just swallow. Trust me, my dear," he added with a smile that heated the air between them.

Carwyn took the shell. "All right." He gave his food one more look before opening his mouth and tipping the creature past his tongue and swallowing in a big gulp. "Hmm." The texture was a bit slimy, yet the flavor was pleasant and the saltiness of it completely different from the few mouthfuls of ocean he'd swallowed while swimming. Something about its interaction with the creature inside its shell made it less sharp and tastier. "I like it."

"Good." Aleki traded the empty shell for a full one, repeating the exchange a few more times until almost half the mollusks were gone. When Carwyn signaled he'd had enough, his husband cut up some kind of tuber and handed it over. "This is better cooked. My mother makes a pie with it for festivals. It will help fill the rest of your belly."

Carwyn bit off a chunk and chewed. It was hard and bland yet with a hint of sweetness. "You must eat, too, Aleki. We need you in top shape when the attack comes." He hadn't used his husband's name very often. It tripped off his tongue easily. Whatever formalness had existed between them was drifting away. It might have taken a long while for that to happen under normal circumstances. Their predicament had forced an emotional intimacy more quickly, at least as far as he was concerned.

"Not to worry. There is plenty here and even more around us." Nevertheless, he downed the rest of the mollusks before joining Carwyn on the rock with half a lily fruit in one hand and a tuber in the other. His proximity helped chase the coldness away because waves of heat emanated from his skin. The man's erection had only half flagged.

And because his arousal was also lingering and he wanted to have some touch, Carwyn scooted closer and pressed his body against his husband's. "Do you think we dare sleep tonight?"

"You will. I won't."

He frowned "That's not—"

"Don't say 'fair'."

Carwyn shot his husband a glare. "Well, it's not."

Aleki chewed a big chunk of the vegetable, then sighed. "Are we going to spend the rest of our married life arguing about the sensible decisions I make?"

"Probably, because I have not yet agreed that any decision you make is automatically sensible compared to my point of view. I am not brainless — and neither is Nora, so don't think you would have been better off with her. If you want a wife who never questions you, you'll have to seek one elsewhere." He squealed when his husband grabbed him by the back of the neck and hauled him closer for a kiss. It was little more than a peck — a hard one, though, and it caused his flagging erection to come roaring back.

Aleki gave him a hooded look. "I want no other wife but you, which is why I insist that you sleep while I guard you. When they come for us, it will be a brutal fight for our lives. It's important that you are as fit as you can be. I, of course, am a seasoned warrior and used to going without sleep for days. Remember that long before the Swarm, my people have battled pirates for generations. My skill and tactics weren't learned from a book and practiced only during training. Can you say the same?" he added before Carwyn could mount a retort.

His husband had him there. "Okay." Giving in to the man wasn't so hard, and there really wasn't much of a choice…any choice. He needed the sleep. He'd been so busy during the day, it had been easy to ignore tiredness and soreness. Now, the food and the inactivity allowed his fatigue to set in, and there wasn't a muscle in his body that didn't scream with the need to relax. He wasn't sure he could manage to take a turn watching for problems, given his condition. And it wasn't as if he had the power to make Aleki rest. "You're right."

His husband nodded once before going back to eating. He was also fully hard once more and seeing the cock jutting out from between Aleki's thighs gave Carwyn an idea. There was something he could do to help the man relax at least. Knowing that Aleki would almost certainly refuse, Carwyn didn't bother to ask. Instead, he stood and maneuvered onto his knees and elbowed his husband's brawny legs apart. He slid both hands up Aleki's thighs until his thumbs rested against the man's balls.

Aleki froze, then coughed once before saying, "What are you doing, wife?"

Carwyn looked up at him from under his lashes. "Easing the tension of the day, husband."

"That's not...*oh*." Aleki grunted the last word out as Carwyn stuck out his tongue to lick the underneath of that magnificent dick.

"Hmm." Attending to the cock this way was a treat. His husband had given him the pleasure of a blow job a few times since their wedding yet had discouraged him from reciprocating. He'd said he wanted to take their love-making slower than that, a silly goal that made no sense to Carwyn. He was no stranger to sucking cock and enjoyed doing so. He wanted to bring his husband this pleasure.

"This isn't necessary." The man's words were strangled and not as forceful as usual.

Sensing that his husband was about to nevertheless put a stop to things, Carwyn upped the game by sliding his tongue through the slit. It was already full of pre-cum. The taste reminded Carwyn of the mollusks. *Maybe that's why I enjoyed them.* He deliberately moaned to show his appreciation. Aleki had to understand that this was not a chore. Shuffling closer, he opened his mouth to take in the cock's head. At the same time, he cupped the heavy balls with one hand and clasped the shaft with the other. He knew what a man liked and had developed some skill in doing this. There was no chance that he could swallow Aleki's long, thick dick, so he concentrated on working all the places he could manage—massaging the balls, jerking the shaft and sucking on the head with real enthusiasm. The fun didn't last, however. The twitching of Aleki's cock and his increasingly labored breathing gave fair warning. When cum exploded into his mouth, Carwyn was ready for it, swallowing quickly and keeping up with all of his efforts until he'd milked his husband dry.

Carwyn licked his lips, then grinned. "How was that?"

"Hah! I think you know the answer already." Aleki smiled while he ran his fingers through Carwyn's hair. "You have a great talent, my dear. I am a lucky man. Now stand up."

He didn't hesitate to do so, having made his point, and curious about what his husband intended. His own cock was achingly hard. Being jerked to a climax would be fine by him. Aleki had other ideas, however. Gripping Carwyn's ass, he brought him in closer, then squeezed the lily fruit half he still held. Juice dribbled onto and down Carwyn's dick. He couldn't hold back the gasp of delight. That sound turned to a low moan when his husband dropped the rind to take a tight hold on his ass with both hands, his large fingers pressing into his flesh. He lifted him practically onto his toes to line his cock up to Aleki's mouth. He consumed the dick as if slurping a mollusk from its shell. This was how it always was, his husband having no trouble taking the entirety of Carwyn's cock, although this time, he used his tongue to tease along the shaft. Carwyn dug into the man's shoulders as the orgasm washed over him. Aleki swallowed him down to the root and worked the dick with this throat until Carwyn collapsed against his husband.

Aleki scooped him up into his arms as he stood. "Now it's time to sleep, wife. Please let yourself do so, secure that I watch over you."

"I know you'll protect me." His voice had a dreamy quality, even to his own ears, because he was halfway to passing out. Aleki lowered him onto the soft ferns he'd used to make a pallet, then covered him with some others. It was easy to let himself drift off. Whatever was coming, Aleki would be there to protect him. And they would defeat the mutineers. They had to.

Chapter Seven

Despite the harsh conditions, Carwyn appeared to sleep the untroubled kind of a child. The fact that he'd dropped off quickly and never awoke during the night proved far better than words that the boy was sure his husband would watch over him and keep him safe. Aleki hated seeing his wife in such dire circumstances and felt the failure to protect him from this entire calamity deep in his bones. If he allowed it, the emotion would consume him. But that wasn't what would help Carwyn. To prevail this day, Aleki needed the cold, hard focus of a warrior. He had to push aside the softer feelings that kept trying to bubble to the surface. They were difficult to face in any event because he hadn't expected to fall in love with his wife. And yet as he crouched beside Carwyn, he knew that was what was happening.

Reluctantly, he touched his wife's shoulder. "Time to wake up, my dear."

The boy's eyes fluttered open and once they landed on Aleki, he sat up quickly. "Are they here?"

Hating the sound of fear in his wife's voice, Aleki worked to keep him calm. "Not yet but they are coming. I spotted the yawl rounding the point. It's heading toward the sandy beach that I anticipated they would make as their landing point."

Carwyn rubbed the sleep from his eyes. "Thank the gods you were right about that."

"Yes. Our plan will work. Here, eat some of this." He handed him a half of a lily fruit.

Carwyn took it but frowned. "I'm not hungry."

"I understand. You must try, though. The prospect of fighting ties the stomach in knots, but a lack of food will make you weak when you need your strength the most."

His wife gratified him by taking small bites. "There's a flaw in our plan, you know. I thought to say something when you outlined it but didn't want to contradict you, given how much you dislike my questioning you." He rolled his eyes with a small grin to show he wasn't looking to pick a fight. "Now that I've slept on it, I'm sure I'm right."

This didn't bode well. "How so?" As he asked the question, he feared he knew what the answer was because of course, he'd also seen the problem, even as he'd laid out what they would do.

Carwyn squirmed a bit before replying, his gaze focused on the fruit he was no longer nibbling on. "You can't lead them to the traps. They won't fall for the ruse if it's you they are chasing." He looked at him now. "Kai Aleki would never be caught unaware by his enemies then run away. That's something a helpless wife would do."

Both pleased that the boy was so clever and vexed at what he was proposing, Aleki could only shake his head. "No." He stood and went to the rocky lookout of their redoubt. The dot he'd spotted earlier in the ocean was getting closer. "I will not risk you that way."

Carwyn came to stand by his side, too short to see over the rocky ledge, yet just the right size to hug Aleki's waist. "If they kill you, I won't last here for very long. My only hope of living is if you are protected enough to attack them. I'm good with a bow, but not so much that I can get them all when they charge me. I'm not sure I have the fortitude to do it, either. I'm still queasy over knifing that sailor and I didn't even deliver the killing blow."

Aleki closed his eyes on a sigh. He shouldn't be surprised that his wife was smart enough and sufficiently trained in warfare that he'd flushed out the flaws of the plan. It was damn irritating. "I would wish to spare you from more violence. We cannot afford to give them any quarter. If even one of them survives, he will be a continuing danger to us and the rest of my loyal crew."

"You're making my case for me. I don't trust myself to be as ruthless as is necessary. But I do know that I can act afraid—mostly because I am. When they chase after me, their guard will be down, hopefully. Easy pickings for you."

Aleki hugged his wife close, hating that he was right. "You're a fast runner?"

"Very. When you grow up with three older siblings that you can't resist teasing, you learn to be."

He smiled at that bit of information. "You will have to tell me more...when this is over." Sighing, he pressed a kiss to the top of his wife's head. "Come. We'll go over the path so that I'm sure you know where the traps are."

"If it eases your worry."

"Well, it will help keep my head from exploding as I picture you out there taunting Rei's men." The frank admission surprised him. He should have been embarrassed to show such weakness. Instead, he felt oddly...anchored, as if Carwyn had become his port of calm. There was no chance to dwell on it, however. Time was not on their side. "We must hurry." With that, he led his wife from the relative safety of the rock and into the dangerous jungle.

* * * *

Staying naked had been Carwyn's idea, and while his husband's effort to remain calm had been obvious, the warrior in him had readily seen the value of it, even if the husband in him rebelled at the notion. Men were easy to distract with an enticing body, and Carwyn knew that he had one. Men had been giving him sideways glances long before they should have. Rei's men had to be tired and irritated with their search, and the thought of sampling their kai's wife before carting them both back to the ship would hopefully make them think more with their dicks than their heads. If they were sufficiently distracted, they wouldn't have time to consider the wisdom of charging after him.

He could see the yawl now, populated with six men rowing over the breakers, as Aleki had predicted. And it was only the one. It took a lot of crew to man a sailing war ship, and with half the men either dead or imprisoned, the bastard Rei couldn't afford to send two or more boats after them. The constraint had bought them time to set their defenses. Carwyn could only hope that they'd succeed. *It's up to me.*

It was torturous to wait for the enemy to first land their boat, then disembark and decide amongst themselves how to proceed. There were no tracks to follow as Aleki had deemed laying down some too obvious a ploy. Instead, Carwyn had to wait behind some trees along the most likely path for the search party to take. Swaying from one foot to the other, with hands he opened and closed hanging against his thighs, Carwyn took in deep breaths to steady his racing heart. *Come on. Come on.* Finally, the waiting was over. The six men started toward the edge of the jungle, five of them carrying swords and the sixth a bow with a quiver of arrows at his back. That was the one who worried him the most. Aleki had surmised that at least one of their pursuers would be an archer. The Chainers didn't use them as much as the Moorcondian army did, but they came in handy when fighting on both a ship and on land. Carwyn was fairly confident in his ability to keep ahead of these men when they chased him. Arrows were harder to avoid. It was a calculated risk. Aleki was sure that Rei wouldn't allow his men to kill them unless absolutely necessary. They were too valuable alive. But in the heat of the moment, these tired and angry warriors might take the more expedient route. There was no hope for it. The course of action had been set. Time for him to kick it off.

Carwyn grabbed the two lily fruits that he'd put by his feet, then paced forward, waiting for the moment when he'd be spotted. It didn't take long. The man leading the cohort of warriors caught sight of him and let out a cry. Carwyn made himself hesitate, let them get a good look, tried to express surprise and fear before letting out his own scream. He dropped the fruit, turned and ran. The vegetation littering the ground stung the soles of his bare feet, yet he paid the discomfort no mind. Worse pain waited for him if he failed, and the thought of Aleki being sold to the Swarm for a blood sacrifice gave him the best incentive of all to fly his way toward the first trap. Behind him, Rei's men whooped and hollered, commanding him to stop. When the first trap came into view, it goosed his spirit. This might be the best test of who would emerge victorious this day.

He hoped he'd kept enough distance between him and his pursuers for them not to notice that he skirted the scattered fronds, stones and sticks Aleki had laid over the trap. Surely these men were trained to do such things, too, and could spot what had been done. But if they didn't see him dodge the area and if he presented enough of a distraction... Carwyn had his answer moments later when screams reached him as he fled. It was tempting to look over his shoulder, yet he didn't. Aleki had warned him that doing such a thing slowed one down when running, and he couldn't afford to lose any ground. At least two men had died, of that he was certain — maybe more — and he tried not to picture the broken bodies impaled on the wicked spikes his husband had whittled. This was a war, and it was either them or Rei's men who would prevail — and that meant killing the enemy.

The shouting intensified as he sprinted toward the redoubt where Aleki waited for him. Furious invectives were hurled at his back, threats of violence against him being used as verbal clubs. It was silly, really, that they thought promising vengeance on him would cause him to stop and surrender. He was hopeful that their rage would make them more careless instead of careful. Putting on speed, he leaped over a fallen log and the small trap just beyond it. An arrow whizzed past his head, causing him to stumble and cry out. He managed to keep himself upright, but his heart hammered painfully, and his lungs started to burn as he worked to pick up speed again. His pursuers might have been able to catch up to him from that brief slowdown alone, except the second trap sprung. Once again, he knew he'd succeeded only from the sounds the man made as his foot became ensnared and his body flung against the tree where Aleki had secured another stake. Carwyn's stomach lurched at the mere thought of the impalement. Still, he pressed on and soon saw his destination.

The mere thought of reaching the safety of being at Aleki's side gave him a burst of energy. As he hit the rocky incline, another arrow flew past this head. This time, it was heading away from him, and a muted grunt let him know that his husband had hit his mark. Carwyn scrambled up to the protective ring of boulders and practically threw himself behind Aleki's broad body. He wanted to hug the man, but it wasn't the time or place for affection or relief. They were now under attack. He sat with his back against the rock where Aleki had positioned himself and worked to regain his breath.

The ping of something hitting the other side of their natural barricade made it impossible for him to remain quiet. "H-how many are there?"

Crouching just below the top of the rock, Aleki glanced at him. "I've spotted two of them left. Did six land or were there more hidden in the yawl?"

"It was only the six. Just as you thought. Two fell into the pit, I believe, and one was taken out by the snare." Once again, his stomach rebelled at the unbidden vision of wooden spikes tearing through flesh. He pushed the queasiness down with a hard swallow.

"I shot their archer because he was getting too close to you, and I didn't trust his aim. The arrow he let loose came too close to your head. Another took up those arms in his place, so we are pinned down for the moment. This is not an unexpected outcome. Rei would have been foolish to send only warriors carrying swords, although I had hoped he would, given the limited space in the yawl. No matter," he added with a sigh. "We will implement the back-up plan."

This eventuality didn't surprise Carwyn. He'd never truly believed that they would be able to take them all out that easily. That was okay. He was good with a bow and was confident he could keep the attackers occupied while Aleki circled around them. Holding out his hand, he said "I'll make sure their attention stays on me."

Aleki hesitated before handing the weapon over. "Remember to shoot through the crevice. We want them to believe I'm still here, and if they catch sight of your pretty golden hair, they'll know I'm not."

Carwyn tossed his head, ridiculously pleased at the casual complement, not that he felt attractive at the moment with the strands wet with sweat. "Don't worry. I know what to do. You just make sure you don't fall off the rocks. If you die and leave me with this problem, I'll be very cross." He smiled and batted his eyes.

Aleki grinned, as intended, and gave him a quick hard kiss before racing in a crouch to the far end of the redoubt. He'd fashioned a rope from vines and anchored it to a skinny rock. The strength of the whole thing looked dubious to Carwyn, yet his husband had assured him it would hold his weight. Because watching would only make him more anxious, he turned back to his own role. The slender crevice between two large boulders gave him enough room to send an arrow through. It wouldn't hit anything, but that wasn't the point. Distraction was. The crude bow was hard to use, stiff and unyielding without his putting every ounce of strength into it. He'd practiced a bit the day before and knew he could manage it. When he let loose the first arrow, he knew a moment's satisfaction that fled as soon as a voice called out.

"Kai Aleki, we know you're up there and are trapped. We won't waste more of our arrows shooting at rocks, and we won't run into our own slaughter, either. Easier for us to wait you out. We have plenty of food and water to gather. How long can you last without access to any of that? You can blame your foolish kailisa for leading us right to you. Surrender to us now, and we'll give you a chance to beat him for his mistake before we rape him. We are owed that much reward, given the fate of our comrades."

Carwyn was tempted to launch another arrow but stayed the impulse. Aleki would never allow himself to be baited like that. Instead, he stuck his tongue out—childish and hidden from view, yet it made him feel better. He stayed pressed against the rock, straining to hear any sign that Aleki had managed to come up behind them. It was futile, he knew. Walking silently was second nature to his husband. He could only hope that their enemy weren't any better at detecting his approach than Carwyn was himself. Although he tried not to think about it, the part that worried him was that Aleki was armed with only a knife. He'd have to get very close to his quarry in order to kill him—and there were two. What if Aleki took out one of the men and was attacked by the other?

Stop borrowing trouble. He knows what he's doing.

No sooner than he'd thought that than a yell reached him. Then there was the clash of steel. With an arrow notched, Carwyn dared to creep around the side of the boulder and peer down into the jungle. What he saw caused his breath to catch in his throat. One man was down with the bow and arrows strewn beside his corpse. Of course Aleki had been smart enough to kill him first. And he must have taken the man's sword, because he was battling the remaining warrior with it. Each time those pieces of steel crashed against each other, Carwyn's nerves jumped. And he remained ready to let an arrow lose himself if Aleki appeared to be losing. As it was, the two men danced around too much for him to dare to take the shot.

He knew a moment of sheer panic when his husband fell to one knee. But he needn't have worried. Intended or not, the position gave Aleki an opening to stab the sword into his opponent's belly before rolling away. Rei's warrior sliced nothing but air as he staggered and fell onto his face. It was done. They had survived the battle with the search party. They weren't yet victorious, though. The tougher part was ahead of them. He couldn't dwell on that, however. With his bow and arrow clasped in one hand, he raced down the slope and plowed into his husband.

"You did it!"

Aleki wrapped his free arm around him and hugged him tight, while scanning the area. "*We* did it, my dear. Still, I must be sure the others are truly dead. Go and gather our kilts and the other knives. We need to leave on the next tide and let the cover of darkness help us retake the ship."

"Okay." Needing a moment more of comfort, Carwyn held on to his man. And in that moment, he came to a conclusion. "You, um, heard what they said about me?" When Aleki jerked his head in a nod, Carwyn continued. "I know you're better than Rei or any of his warriors and believe we will retake the ship. But if we don't...if things go against us, I don't intend to let them take me alive. I don't want that fate, and more importantly, I can't bear seeing the one they have planned for you. You'll take care of that for me, won't you? Please?" He hated to ask yet feared he wouldn't be able to go through with it himself.

Aleki said nothing for a long while. He simply held Carwyn tightly against him, the tension running through him being a palpable thing. Finally, he said, "If it comes to that—and I swear to you, it won't—I promise I'll take care of us both."

And with that grim pact having been made, they went about the business of leaving the island.

* * * *

Aleki paused in his gruesome task, swiping the sweat from his brow. Even with the sun setting, he was hot from the effort it had taken to drag all of Rei's dead warriors down to the beach. Retrieving the two from the pit alone had been taxing. Tying them into the yawl in a hideous tableau of rowers had been no mean feat, either. It had to be done. If they approached the ship with only he and Carwyn visible, they'd be set upon immediately. Their only chance was to make it look as if Rei's warriors returned while he and Carwyn clung to the boat unseen. During his training as a warrior, one of his teachers had told the tale of some long ago boarding of an enemy ship being done exactly in this manner. He and the others had found it delightfully grisly, not even sure it wasn't made up. He could only hope that none of Rei's men had heard the same story.

He glanced over to where Carwyn sat on his kilt, spread out on top of a flat rock, keeping watch in case another yawl approached. It was a real concern and an important role, yet it also served to keep the boy from witnessing him dragging bloody corpses and arranging them much as his sister had used to do with her dolls. His own stomach was less than pleased with it all, and he'd seen much of death. But there was no pity in him. These men had betrayed him and their country. They'd pursued him and Carwyn without mercy, so their fates were just. At least they'd died quickly. Even the last two he'd dispatched hadn't suffered…unlike himself. The burns on his hands from the rope he'd used to climb down the rocks stung enough to make his eyes water some, and the soles of his feet hurt, despite their toughness. Worse, he knew his wife was similarly injured, not that Carwyn complained. Aleki had seen him limping, though, and that alone made him long to strangle Rei with his bare hands.

All that being said, he knew Carwyn was disturbed by the killings. Aleki had firmly rejected the offer for help. He wanted to spare his wife as much as possible. The journey back to the boat would be sufficiently hard. Resting now and enjoying the relative calm from the lull in the fighting would hopefully help energize him to face what had to be done once they got back onto the ship. Aleki was willing to break his own back in order to protect his wife's sensibilities. Carwyn was fierce and fearless, but it was Aleki's duty to do the hard stuff in their lives, and right now, that meant tying bodies together in a way that gave the illusion the men sat upright and rowed.

Finally, it was done, and full darkness had descended. It was a cloudy night and that was a blessing. The harder it was to see, the better their chances to reboard the ship undetected. He washed the gore off his hands in the surf before joining his wife. The clever boy greeted him with cut-open lily fruit and a pile of mollusks. "You must be both exhausted and starving."

Aleki sat beside him on his own kilt that Carwyn had laid out for him. The clothing was frayed from their adventures but it hardly mattered. Their swim back was better done without the drag of wet fabric. There was plenty more on the ship to replace it, and once they arrived home, he looked forward to draping his wife with finery. He bit into the fruit to quench his thirst before answering. "It was…difficult work, I admit."

Carwyn grimaced. "You should have let me help you."

"No." There was no point in wasting time, energy or breath in justifying his decision. His wife would have to learn that in some things, he was the master and wouldn't seek Carwyn's approval or understanding.

However much that answer irked the boy, he said nothing, merely opened a mollusk and handed it to him. "Have as much as you like. I've already eaten." Pressing a hand against his stomach, he added, "I don't want a full stomach anyway. The swim back will be difficult."

"Not as hard as the journey here. The yawl will give us stability. Although we'll be pushing it along, so that will be somewhat of an extra strain." Aleki downed the offering and waited for Carwyn to serve him more. This at least must help his wife feel useful. And truth be told, he liked the pampering.

"I'm ready for whatever, and that includes the fight once we free your men. Oh, don't scowl at me," he added with his own. "I'm not helpless. I've been trained as a soldier, remember?"

"I do." He hated to admit it, but it was good that his wife knew how to fight, even if he wanted to secret him away until it was safe to come out in the open. "I won't stop you from wielding a sword with me and my men, but you'll do so from somewhere other than the front lines."

"That's sensible. You and your warriors are better suited to lead the charge anyway. And I won't take stupid chances."

Aleki paused his eating and shot his wife a reassuring smile. "I know you won't. You've been clever and brave. I am a lucky man."

"Yes, you are," Carwyn agreed with a toss of his head. There was silence while Aleki stuffed his face, the effort of the last few hours making him starving, as Carwyn had observed. Then, his wife surprised him with a request. "Before we leave, would you do me a favor?"

"I will always give you what's in my power to do so." He couldn't imagine what the request was going to be, but he intended to fulfill it.

"Fuck me before we leave...please."

Aleki was part shocked and part amused and rendered speechless, an almost unheard-of occurrence with him. "Fuck you?"

Carwyn wrinkled his nose. "I was going to say make love to me, but I don't think we have time for that."

Aleki's cock tried to answer for him. Pressing his palm over it in a futile gesture to hide it, he leaned toward his wife. "It is not simply a matter of time, my dear. There is no oil here to ease my way, and I won't hurt you." He placed his free hand on Carwyn's knee. The skin was as smooth as ever and cool, despite the still-simmering heat. "When we have retaken the ship and on our way to my homeland, I will worship your body as you deserve."

Carwyn shook his head. "I can't wait." He looked away before continuing. "I don't mind a little discomfort. In fact, it's exactly what I do want—to feel you inside me as we make our journey back." The boy stared at him once more with shining eyes. "The reminder of whom I belong to and the power you wield will…anchor me. *Please,*" he added again, and this time, he moved to climb into Aleki's lap.

The boy's touch fried Aleki's already tired brain. He opened his mouth to voice once more his reasonable objections. The words stuck in his throat as his wife pressed his hard dick against Aleki's fist. Then a groan pushed past his lips, and his control started to unravel. He released his grip on his cock, freeing the hard length and allowing him to wrap Carwyn in his arms. Their lips met in an unspoken need to ravish each other's mouths. Never entirely shy and reticent while having sex, Carwyn turned into the aggressor, twining his tongue with Aleki's and humping in a fast undulation of his hips. If he kept that movement up much longer, Aleki was going to come too soon.

He broke the kiss and pulled his wife to his feet. "Let us at least find a more comfortable spot." He walked away from the rocky shore with his kilt in hand, looking for a pile of fronds. The sand would be hard on Carwyn's skin, even covered by cloth. Thankfully, a patch was easy to find just past the tree line. He spread his kilt down like a blanket, then claiming his wife's mouth once more, he lowered him onto it.

Aleki loved seeing Carwyn's face when they had sex, but it would be easier on the boy's body if he kneeled instead of lying down. And taking him from behind would give Aleki more control. With only spit as a lubricant, he'd have to be careful.

Understanding his intent, his wife didn't resist when he turned him around and positioned him on his hands and knees. Carwyn leaned on his elbows, widened his legs and lifted his pert ass in the air. It was irresistible. Still, Aleki took it slowly, placing himself between those legs and teasing Carwyn's hole with one wet finger. It took so little to invade the boy, his puckered ring opening without any resistance. When he slid his finger in up to the last knuckle and twisted it, Carwyn moaned in encouragement. Aleki amused them both by thrusting steadily, then he crooked his finger and scraped against his wife's prostate.

Carwyn cried out and bucked against the thrusting. He clenched his hole, providing resistance as Aleki pulled his finger out. More spit allowed him to use two fingers, and he bent over to clasp Carwyn's dick. A few thrusts and jerks made the boy come. Carwyn's cries startled birds around them. Aleki caught some of the boy's cum and coating his cock with it, pressed into that tight channel. Knowing the prep and lubricant wasn't enough to ease his way, he tried to stay still once he'd bottomed out, but Carwyn didn't let him. The boy snapped his hips to fuck himself with Aleki's cock, a clear demand that Aleki ride him hard and fast. He didn't need much convincing. Grabbing hold of his wife's hips, he pounded into that welcoming ass. His climax ripped through him within seconds. He pulled Carwyn's backside tightly against his pelvis and held him there. He wanted to remember this moment, needed to, when he returned to his ship to retake it. This was why he fought—for this boy, his wife.

I love him. The thought didn't scare him, but it did energize him. He would not fail his wife. He would get Carwyn safely to his new home. Then he would rain terror on the Swarm for daring to think they could hurt his boy.

Chapter Eight

The journey back to the ship was both easier and harder than their escape. It seemed as if it had been ages ago instead of less than two days. Aleki took the brunt of the effort to guide the yawl back with its dead crew. He pushed from the stern, careful to keep the small ship between him and Carwyn and the larger vessel. The cloudy sky was helping, but keen eyes with a spyglass could still make them out if they didn't hide behind the barrier. Every so often, he allowed himself to flick his gaze at his wife. Carwyn stuck valiantly by his side, helping to push it along. Aleki admired the boy's efforts to be of use instead of just assuming Aleki would do everything. But Aleki was also determined to keep him from having to overtax himself. For someone who wasn't a warrior, the Moorcondian had proved his mettle. Still, there was worse to come, and Carwyn needed to conserve his energy. They didn't talk because the water had a way of carrying sounds, so all Aleki could do was subtly encourage his wife to take it as easy as he could—not that the stubborn boy seemed to be complying.

He didn't try to be quiet while swimming. In fact, he'd told his wife before they'd set out to not worry about splashing as they swam. The sound would help add to the illusion that Rei's men were actually rowing. He'd tied the oars on the wrists of the corpses, keeping them hovering above the water to avoid creating a drag. It was entirely possible that the elaborate set-up was doomed to failure. His loyal men would be too well-trained to fall for such a ruse. They would never let a yawl return without keeping a keen eye on its approach to make sure it held no one hostile. He was banking on Rei's men having been picked because they were easily coopted and not due to their warrior skills.

When they were close enough that he could see the deck in more detail, he scanned for sentries and found only two on that side of the boat. Neither of them was paying much attention, although one did raise a hand as if in greeting. Stupid. The dead men had their backs to the bow in typical rowing style. Even if they'd been alive, they wouldn't see anything on the ship. Their lack of response was explainable. Aleki relaxed a fraction. This was the first test. If one of the sentries had hailed them verbally, it would have been difficult to answer as if he were in the boat. As that didn't happen, he had one less thing to worry about—for the moment. A short while later, he judged they were within easy swimming distance. He tapped Carwyn on the shoulder, their pre-agreed-to signal that the boy should break away and head for the far side of the ship. Aleki kept the yawl on its course until he saw his wife's head bobbing beside the same rope ladder hanging over the side of the ship that they'd used to make their escape in the first place. That was another mistake. It should have been hauled up. Then he gave the yawl one last big shove before diving below the surface and swimming underwater to his wife's side.

There was no time to linger. Soon the ruse would be discovered, and they'd lose the element of surprise. This was the moment of greatest danger. If they were discovered before managing to free his men, there would be no hope of success. And that meant he'd be forced to fulfill his promise to his wife to keep him from falling into Rei's vicious hands. The very thought of killing his darling boy roiled his stomach. *So make sure it doesn't come to that.* Wasting no more time dwelling on a failure he wouldn't permit, Aleki grabbed hold of the rope and shimmied up. He pulled out the two knives he'd tied to each thigh with scraps from his kilt. The short blades would be no match against a sword, but if he were careful and quick—two of his best skills—he could take out any threat before the warriors pulled out their own weapons.

Carwyn proved once again that he was strong and capable, joining him in short order and only slightly out of breath. Aleki didn't hesitate to begin creeping their way to the stairs. As he did so, he scanned the deck and was surprised to see that the two sentries he'd spied were the only ones on duty. Not being a warrior himself, Rei had underestimated the manpower needed for such a large vessel. His mutineers were spread thin, and the man had failed to appreciate how much a threat Aleki was. He changed plans in the blink of an eye. Signaling Carwyn to stay put, he raced to the nearest look-out. He shoved one knife back into its make-shift sheath, used the now-free hand to cover his target's mouth then plunged his other weapon into the man's back. It was over in moments, and a quick glance at the far end of the ship told him the other guard was focused on watching the approaching yawl and had missed his companion being taken out.

Aleki could tell when the guy had finally realized something was up with the small ship of corpses. There was no time to waste. He went to grab the dead sentry's bow, only to find that his wife had been disobedient. Carwyn already had it in his hands. The boy notched an arrow and let it fly just as the other man turned to call out. It was an impressive shot, spearing him in the throat. The warrior dropped with a faint gurgling sound carrying over the deck. Carwyn briefly grinned at Aleki, conflicting emotions flashing across his lovely face. It pained Aleki that his wife had now been forced to kill, but he appreciated that Carwyn was in no small way helping to free his men. He owed the boy a debt of gratitude, but there would be time to dwell on that later.

Grabbing the dead sentry's sword, he proceeded with the original plan and crept downstairs. There was no one stirring, which again, was foolish on Rei's part. If he'd expected his two guards on deck to sound the alarm if trouble arrived, he'd been a poor judge of their skills. And now, that inadequacy gave Aleki and Carwyn a clear path to the hold where his men were imprisoned. Before they reached their destination, however, his wife surprised him yet again. With a grab of Aleki's arm, Carwyn stopped him and held out the bow and quiver of arrows he'd taken off the dead man. Aleki cocked his head, not quite sure what his wife was trying to say or do., He had no choice but take the weapons as well as the two knives the boy pulled out, one from his leather thigh sheath and the other he'd fashioned from his scarf. Carwyn then stripped those holders from his legs and lay them silently on the floor. Before he could figure out Carwyn's intended move, the infuriating minx passed him and walked through the doorway.

"Hi there. Want some company? I got tired of living like a savage and want back into civilization."

Aleki nearly cracked his jaw hearing his wife speaking coyly to another man, putting himself in danger. But a quick look around the hatchway confirmed that he wasn't nearly as knowledgeable about men as Carwyn was. Instead of raising the alarm, the moron left guarding his men stood wide-eyed, practically drooling at the vision of a lithe, naked boy. No, that wasn't quite true. Carwyn did wear something—the bonding bracelet that he'd given him on their wedding day. Despite the fighting, swimming and general fleeing from danger, the symbol of their bond still remained securely on his wife's wrist. It gleamed in the light of the dim lanterns as Carwyn had his hand on the man's arm. The sight of both the bracelet and the touching caused a fierceness to well up inside him. When Carwyn maneuvered the guard so that his back was to the entrance, Aleki raced over and dealt with the fucker as he'd done the sentry on deck. He had to drop the unnecessary weapons to do so, but there was no one around to hear the clatter, and it served to rouse those of his men who hadn't already woken from the sound of Carwyn's voice.

He couldn't help baring his teeth at the body lying at his feet. Then he gave into the impulse to pull his wife to him and swat him on his cute ass with a level of heat that proved to them both how furious he was. "Do not *ever* put yourself in such danger again!" He let his anger, which was born from fear, come through his hushed tone as much as it had with the smack, and he stared as sternly as he could for emphasis.

Carwyn merely rolled his eyes. "It worked, didn't it? I keep telling you men think with their dicks."

Because there was no comeback that wouldn't sound foolish, Aleki gave up his anger and worry and turned to the pressing matter of freeing his men. As with before, the keys to the cages were nowhere to be found. Rei still wasn't a complete idiot or entirely lax in his governing of the ship, apparently. The sword Aleki had acquired proved useful in breaking the first padlock open now that he was on the outside of the cage and had leverage. He enjoyed a brief reunion with his men before doling out the few weapons they'd secured. If they were going to prevail in retaking the ship, however, they needed more. "Make your way to the armory while I free the others," he ordered with his focus on Lono. This was the warrior he counted on the most.

Carwyn joined them, wisely keeping his ass out of reach, and held out his hand. "Let me have the sword. I'll free the others while you go ahead. We can't risk having you trapped here, and your men need you to lead them."

There was a general murmur of agreement. His wife was too smart by half. All Aleki could envision at first was that Carwyn would be the one trapped if things went to shit. But there was no denying the wisdom of the suggestion. He gave a quick nod of assent before training his gaze on the most senior warrior yet to be freed. "You keep him safely among you — and give him your kilt." That last order came to him because Carwyn was entirely too fetching and something deep and possessive within him goaded him into making sure his wife stopped flashing his pretty parts to all and sundry. He told himself it was a good strategy for the battle, making sure his men weren't distracted. The truth was he was driven by jealousy, a new and disturbing feeling that he would have to ponder later.

The man bowed. "Yes, kai. No one will touch your kailisa. This I swear." And although the order had been given to the one man, the others followed suit. Their loyalty to his wife as well as to him gave him pride and renewed purpose. With one last glance at Carwyn, he led his men out.

* * * *

Carwyn didn't mind relinquishing the sword and the job of freeing the others to the burly warrior charged with keeping him safe. Breaking the second lock had proven to require a lot of strength, and his hands still stung...as did his ass. He didn't know whether to be miffed or aroused by his husband's swift and brief punishment. It made him wonder if he'd enjoy spanking as part of sex. If it were something they both agreed to and liked, it might be quite thrilling. But if his husband thought to mete out that sort of thing whenever he was mad at him...well, they were going to have a *frank* talk. Carwyn wasn't going to stand for such high-handed treatment. He was affable by nature but not meek and didn't intend to spend their marriage worried about his husband's anger.

Not that he was the least worried about Aleki being mad at the moment. The ploy of distracting the guard with his body had been an obvious one, something that he'd thought of even before they'd left the island. It only made sense to utilize his skills, such as they were, and he'd always been good at seduction. He'd said nothing to his husband, of course. The man was too protective of him to think like a warrior chief, and that impulse couldn't be indulged. There was too much at stake. It wasn't merely about their lives or those of his men. The fate of their countries was at stake. They couldn't let Rei's treachery succeed. He didn't hesitate, either, to accept the warrior's offering of his less than fresh kilt. It wouldn't do to show open defiance of Aleki's authority, and the shyness the warrior showed as he held out the cloth was disarming. It would be like kicking a puppy if he refused.

As he wrapped the clothing around his waist, he stood in a corner to keep out of the way. The area of the hold outside the cages shrunk considerably as the men piled into it. When the last of Aleki's warriors were freed, there was a noticeable excitement among them. Even though they had only the one sword, each one acted as he were armed to the teeth. They didn't hesitate to leave the hold, managing to cocoon him as they did so, protecting him from all sides. He didn't mind. If he never had to lift another finger to fight, he'd be happy. Killing the sentry had been necessary, a duty he hadn't shirked from — but he'd hated it. Every time the image of the arrow piercing the man's neck popped into his head, he banished it again. Dwelling on the nastiness of the situation wasn't helpful. The sweet ache deep inside his ass helped to center him, too. As he'd expected, the lingering feel of Aleki's mounting him was like carrying a piece of the man with him. Silly perhaps, but there it was. *I do love him. If – no, when – this whole thing is over, I must tell him.* He also told himself it didn't matter if his husband didn't love him back. Just because he didn't now, there was no reason to fear that he never would.

The sounds of the vicious fight that had broken out reached them before they'd gone upstairs to the deck. The armed men went first, jumping into the bloody fray with warrior cries that caused his blood to freeze. Trapped as he was between two burly warriors, Carwyn had to rise on tiptoes to spot Aleki. He was easy to find even so, large and impressive, his loose hair flying as he pivoted between two opponents. His straining muscles gleamed in the moonlight that had finally pushed through the clouds. Carwyn's first instinct was to go to him, to even up the fight. But two of his husband's men who had formed the core of his protection herded him in the opposite direction, toward a relatively quiet corner of the deck. One scooped up a fallen sword, the other a stray knife. It meant slipping through the blood that had spilled onto the deck by two felled men. Carwyn's stomach rebelled at the repulsive visceral feel of it. He was glad he'd eaten lightly before leaving the island and swallowed down the bile. Now was not the time for distracting anyone with a delicate disposition. Instead, he pressed his back against the ship's railing and kept his eye out for sneaky behavior about which he might shout out a warning.

As a boy, he'd relished watching soldiers train, their mock battles being exciting. Now he understood that real war was nothing like those events. This was brutal, horrible, an obscenity that was beyond imagination. He wondered if he would hear the cries of pain and death, smell the stench of blood and guts vomiting out of men's bodies and feel the bone-deep terror of it all for the rest of his life. How did his husband stand doing this even once, let alone seeking it out over and over again? He couldn't fathom it, yet appreciated that because Aleki and others did, he could sleep safely in his bed. No, fighting was never going to be his calling, but he wasn't helpless. When one of his guards fell from a stab to his side, he didn't hesitate to whip off his borrowed kilt and press it against the man's wounds. The other warrior dispatched the attacker before he could use his sword against Carwyn.

Ignoring the clash of swords around him, Carwyn kept the pressure against the warrior's bleeding side, while managing to wrap the rest of the kilt around his waist to tie the make-shift bandage in place. "Sorry," he murmured as he caused the man to grunt.

"Kailisa, please stand back. I am fine." Stubbornness and male pride was apparently part of the warrior training. *No surprise there.* Still, Carwyn helped the man to his feet because someone else bore down on them. Aleki's warrior grabbed the dead man's sword on his way up and lunged with it, even as he shoved Carwyn behind him.

Carwyn slid a fallen knife toward himself with his foot and picked it up quickly. Now that everyone seemed well-armed, he wanted to be as well. With the shifting of the fighting men around the deck, he could easily end up alone and wasn't about to be left helpless. He clutched the knife in a sweaty palm and hid it behind his back. At the same time, he searched for Aleki, his heart pounding with renewed fear when he couldn't spot him where he'd been before. Then relief washed over him at the sight of his husband slashing his sword through the air at a new opponent. Because Carwyn couldn't easily distinguish between the loyal warriors from the traitors, he didn't know if his side was winning or not. Only the almost triumphant look on Aleki's face as he skewered the man he fought gave hope that they were indeed doing well. His husband raced from one fight to another, joining forces with his men in turn, dispatching their foes. The sound of clashing steel diminished while the groans of injured and dying men littering the deck increased.

Aleki climbed to the roof of the pilot house and shouted. "Surrender or die, traitors! You have lost and will have only this one chance to perhaps save your lives. Renounce your allegiance to Rei, and I will argue for leniency." His booming voice, filled with power and certainty, cut through the noise.

Carwyn held his breath, darting his eyes around as he waited to see if his husband's words would be heeded. Fighting slowed, men backing away from each other, then someone threw down his sword and knelt on the deck with a bow. Others followed suit, although a couple gave war cries as they threw themselves at the loyal warriors they fought. Their ends were swift and decisive. Carwyn clenched his fingers around the knife hilt repeatedly as he shifted his focus around to make sure the fight was truly over. Everyone appeared to think so, relaxing their stances somewhat and beginning to corral the traitorous men into a tight circle. But something wasn't quite right. *Where's Rei?* He caught Aleki's gaze, which was now trained on him. His husband started to smile. His expression morphed into outrage, and he bellowed just as Carwyn felt the tip of a sword on his collarbone.

"It is you who must surrender, Aleki! Unless you want to see your slut's blood coat my sword." There was panic under the tone of triumph. But the sharpness of the weapon and its proximity to Carwyn's jugular weren't to be taken lightly.

Aleki jumped onto the deck. He was aroused now, from the fighting. The effect of his hard cock leading his equally hard body added to the awesomeness of the man. He sneered at Rei. "So you are a coward as well as a traitor, cousin. I wish I could say I'm surprised. And if you find the insult galling, stop hiding behind my wife and fight me like a man." Aleki twirled his sword in his hand as he took a few steps toward them. His men gave him a clear path and cheered him on with muted calls.

"Call me whatever you like, *cousin*. Winning is all that counts, and I hold the last card in this game."

No, you don't, fucker. Carwyn didn't think, he merely acted. There was no way he was going to be used as a weak spot for his husband. His life wasn't as important as the survival of their countries, either. He whipped the knife he held from around his back and struck blindly at Rei before dancing away on clumsy feet. He stumbled against the railing and was immediately shoved behind a warrior. Aleki was a blur of movement as he raced to and into Rei, pushing the man to the deck and yanking the sword from his hand.

The traitorous man was howling and clutching at his thigh where Carwyn's knife was stuck in. "You think you've won? All you've done is condemn our people to death and slavery. You can't defeat the Swarm. My way was the only hope we had. You've only prolonged our inevitable defeat, and you'll see that Moorcondian whore ripped apart in the end, anyway. You'd have been safer with me, you stupid bitch," he hurled in Carwyn's direction.

Carwyn clasped his hands behind his back to hide how much he was shaking now that the fight was over. "I'd rather take my chances with the Swarm, asshole."

Aleki shot him a grim look. "No one will touch you, wife." He turned to crouch behind Rei and pulled the knife from the man's thigh without warning.

Blood spurted in its wake and Rei cried out, clutching his hands around the wound. He bared his teeth at Aleki. "Go ahead and finish me. Do it," he ordered when Aleki made no move, only stood and stared down at him with obvious contempt. "Don't have the stomach for it? I'll help. Picture me shoving my cock up your wife's ass the way I intended to. That should give you the right incentive."

"If I wanted to kill you, cousin, I would have already done so. Certainly no one would deny my right as captain of this ship and as husband to the kailisa. But you are first and foremost a traitor to our people. The prima kailisa has the claim on your fate. I will deliver you and the rest of your men to her for punishment. Until then, we'll make sure you live. Secure them in the hold," he shouted to his warriors in general. "And someone tend to my cousin's wounds."

He handed all but one sword over to the man who guarded Carwyn. "I'll see to the kailisa."

"I'm fine, Aleki. I'll just...hey!" The air whooshed from his lungs as his husband hauled him up by his legs and slung him over his shoulder.

"Mind your head, my dear," was all the infuriating man said as he carried him down the hatchway.

Carwyn gave up his struggle and did as he'd been advised. The truth be told, there was something primal and arousing about being carted off by his man. His dick thought so as well, rising to press against Aleki's shoulder. It was no mean feat, given that the rest of his blood supply was rushing to his head. He wasn't surprised that they ended up in the captain's cabin. His husband dumped him on the bed and had him turned with his hips pulled up and his face planted onto the covers in one swift move. *He can't mean to…*

Oh, but he did. Aleki left him for a moment, then was back dribbling something down Carwyn's crack. The man's harsh breathing was testament to how aroused he was. It was no surprise when he pressed his cock against Carwyn's hole and pushed in with one, long thrust. Carwyn gasped and clutched the bedding. He worked to relax his channel to accommodate the sudden invasion. There was some pain, but the exquisite pleasure overrode it. His already tender ass still welcomed Aleki's cock. And when his husband began to thrust with long, fast strokes, Carwyn convulsed in an orgasm that had him biting the bedding. Aleki came soon after, his cock swelling inside Carwyn's channel, and he let out a bellow loud enough for the entire ship to hear. And maybe that was part of the point, confirming that he had control over his wife again and was not one to be crossed. Carwyn didn't mind if he was being used for a calculated purpose. All that mattered was his husband had claimed him in the most pleasurable way possible. More to the point, they'd won. Rei was defeated and Moorcondia and the Southern Chain could proceed with their plans to destroy the Swarm.

He sighed as Aleki gently rearranged him so that he lay on his back and opened his eyes to the sight of his husband looming over him. "Wow." It was all that he could think to say.

Aleki didn't give him a chance to think of something more. Sitting on the side of the bed, he leaned over to kiss him. It was both gentle and passionate, his husband conquering his mouth with his tongue as thoroughly as his cock had taken Carwyn's ass. It left him equally breathless, and when Aleki pulled away, he reached to keep him in place.

Aleki chuckled. "Greedy boy." He pushed Carwyn's hands down and flipped a blanket over him. "It's time for you to rest. I'll have someone bring warm water to wash in when we've secured the ship. And I'll send a salve from our stores of medicine that will help sooth your scraped feet."

Carwyn tried not to pout, understanding that his husband had more pressing matters than comforting his wife. "What about you? I think some of that blood on you is yours." He frowned as he got a good look for the first time. Aleki had at least some scratches from his battles, although thankfully nothing seemed serious.

Aleki flicked at something on his arm. "I'm fine, and I promise to wash myself before touching you again." He grimaced. "Taking you like this before doing so was not well done of me. I just needed—"

"The release. I understand. And you don't hear me complaining, do you?"

Aleki's expression softened. "No. You have borne all this with quiet courage."

Embarrassed by the praise, Carwyn felt his cheeks heat. "I didn't do much."

"When we have a moment to ourselves, my dear, I will catalogue just how much you did do. Now rest."

"All right. I don't want you worrying about me. Oh," he added as his husband headed for the door, "do me a favor."

"If I can."

"Put on a kilt before you leave." He grinned. "I don't like the idea of other men seeing my husband naked any more than you like them getting an eyeful of your wife."

Aleki's mouth dropped open, then he laughed. "Oh, my dear Carwyn. You are a delightful surprise." Nevertheless, the man tugged a kilt out of a drawer and tied it around his waist. With one more smoldering look, he left the cabin.

Carwyn lay there, moving to get into a more comfortably position and enjoying the deep ache in his ass. *Rest.* His husband had issued that as an order, not a request. He wasn't sure he could do such a thing without Aleki by his side. He needed to try, though, and once he closed his eyes, he realized he could do as told easily. As sleep pulled him under, he let go of the fight.

Chapter Nine

Aleki couldn't remember ever being so tired, not even in his early days of training as a warrior, where sleep deprivation was part of the process. But it had been necessary for him to oversee everything—from securing Rei and his traitorous men in the hold to assigning his loyal men to roles and shifts in a manner that guaranteed the ship would function without straining them to the breaking point. So many hands had been lost in the mutiny. There simply weren't enough men to control the ship as there needed to be. His skeleton crew would have to work extra hard if they were to make it home safely. And he wouldn't ask of them anything that he wasn't prepared to do himself. He could grab a few hours of sleep, then return to the deck to relieve his pilot. At least they were finally under way and headed in the right direction.

He entered his cabin as quietly as possible so as not to wake his wife. The sight of the sleeping boy, his fair hair fanned out around his pretty face, lifted his spirits. It might not have been the most practical thing to do, but he'd made sure that someone had delivered warm water and the best healing balm the ship had on hand, as well as food and fresh drinking water. From the looks of things, Carwyn had woken at some point, washed and eaten. It was a good sign that he slept once more. There had been too little slumber in the last few days. At least Aleki could be sure in the knowledge that his wife would be well-rested before they appeared before the prima kailisa. Sleep deprivation wouldn't help with that nerve-racking event.

As quiet as Aleki tried to be, Carwyn still stirred when he approached the bed. The boy gave him a sleepy smile. "Finally."

"You haven't been trying to stay awake for me, have you?" Guilt already threatened to swamp him. It was his duty to protect his kailisa, and he'd failed in spectacular fashion. The only bright spot was that they'd retaken the ship, and Carwyn hadn't suffered too much injury during the entire mutiny and subsequent battles.

Carwyn stretched his arms. "I have, as it happens. But I was too tired."

"No small wonder, given everything you've suffered."

"It was no more than you did, and you've been working this whole time, haven't you?"

"Of course, I'm the kai. My men needed direction and support. I do have a little time to catch some sleep if I may join you?"

By way of answer, his wife flicked the covers off and wiggled closer to the wall. The sight of the boy's lithe body almost made him forget how tired he was. Except now he had the time to look closely at all the creamy skin, and he saw scratches on Carwyn's lower legs and feet that he hadn't noticed before when they were fighting for survival. He frowned. "You are cut up more than I thought. Did you use any of the salve I had sent?"

Carwyn shrugged. "It's not that bad, and to be honest, I used what little energy I had to eat."

Aleki frowned. "That won't do." He picked up the pot of medicine and sat on the side of the bed with it. "I will tend to you myself."

Carwyn sighed. "You don't need to do that."

"There we disagree, and my opinion in this matter counts for more." As carefully as he could, he lifted the closest foot and placed it on his thigh. On closer inspection, the damage wasn't as bad as he'd feared, especially on the soles.

"I suppose if I try to object anymore, you'll just turn me over and smack my ass."

Aleki couldn't keep the grin off his face. "Now there's a thought." He dipped two fingers into the pot and gently smeared the salve around the boy's ankle. He didn't have to look at his wife to know he was frowning.

"I suppose you think that's a perfectly all right thing for you to do."

It was not unexpected that his wife would bring this subject up—and rightly so. "Not normally." He moved on to the top of the foot, enjoying touching the boy, even like this. He let the silence stretch out and slid his fingers on to the bottom, hating the way Carwyn jerked and suppressed a hiss. Seeing the harm done, allowing himself to acknowledge the dark emotions swirling inside him, he let out his thoughts. "I was scared, you know."

"Oh, Aleki, of course you were. Rei's plans to turn you over for sacrifice to the Swarm would frighten any sane person."

He shook his head with a chuckle, amazed at how his wife could be so perceptive of many things, yet not about that which mattered the most. "Not about me, sweet boy." Gently laying the first foot down, he shifted onto the bed to make it easier to pick up the other one. "I'm a warrior. Death is something I have accepted long ago. It was you that I worried about. I'm surprised you don't understand that by now." He flicked his gaze up to his wife. "You could have died at any time. The swim to the island alone was dangerous. Then running from Rei's men, dodging arrows." He shook his head again. "It freezes my blood just thinking about it."

"Weren't you listening when I said about a million times I was trained as a soldier? All Moorcondian boys are, to some degree or other. Just because I longed for a role at court and was willing to take my cousin's place doesn't mean I'm not good at fighting. I did pretty well, don't you think?"

Aleki paused with his fingers sandwiching Carwyn's narrow foot. "You were magnificent. I have never been so proud of anyone in my life. But it was hard for me to let you do what you did. I failed you as a husband. I did," he insisted as Carwyn opened his mouth. "My duty is to protect you, and I let Rei slip past my sense of danger. It's unforgivable."

"Now you're being stupid." Carwyn huffed. "Anyone could see the man was slippery, but a lot of politicians are. You weren't to know he was conspiring with the Swarm. Who would? Even your prima kailisa thought he was loyal, and I bet she doesn't suffer fools gladly."

"*Our* prima kailisa," he gently corrected. "And you are right about that." He put Carwyn' foot down and stood to return the pot to the table. "It doesn't change the fact that when you sashayed your lovely ass over to that guard to distract him, it scraped my last fucking nerve. All my worry for you had built up to a level I could no longer contain. It damn near killed me picturing your running from Rei's men, dodging our traps and their arrows. Then for you to risk your life once more?" He shook his head. "That guard could have easily snapped your neck instead of being seduced by you. I went a bit mad in that moment."

Carwyn gave him a coy look. "Hmm. I suppose I understand...not that I'm saying you have the right to beat me."

Aleki was surprised and chagrined that his wife thought he would. "I'd never hurt you, my dear." He sat again on the edge of the bed and carded Carwyn's hair away from his face. "That swat didn't cause you much pain, did it?"

Carwyn rolled his eyes. "It stung my pride."

"Ah well, I can't guarantee that won't happen again. There will be times when I insist on something you may not like. And I am a man used to being obeyed."

"Hmm. You're lucky you married me, then. If I were Nora, you'd be bleeding heavily from her tongue lashing, if not a crack on the head."

"I consider myself to be the most fortunate of men, my dear, for so many reasons." He leaned down to kiss his wife, sliding in beside him as he did so. When they both needed air, he broke the kiss, snuggled the boy tightly against his body and covered them with the blanket. He cupped the sweet ass they'd been talking about. "Was I too rough earlier, I mean when I brought you back here and mounted you? The fighting..."

"You don't have to explain. I understand what battle does to a man—and no, far from it. I came harder than I can ever remember." The boy slid his hand up Aleki's thigh. "Let me show my appreciation."

Aleki groaned and stopped his wife's efforts. "As delightful as that sounds, I fear I'm too tired for such sport right now." To punctuate his words, he let out a loud yawn.

With his wife tucked tightly against him, he drifted off quickly, but at some point during his brief sleep, he couldn't resist the temptation Carwyn presented. He turned to him with eyes closed and grasping their two hard cocks together in his hand. It took little effort to bring them both to a climax, and with that release, he slept deeply and without worry.

* * * *

"Oh, it's beautiful." Carwyn clutched Aleki's arm as they stood at the railing and the Moorcondian boy got his first clear look at the main island of the Southern Chain.

They'd passed smaller ones on their approach, including the one he'd been born and raised on, the sight of them lightening Aleki's heart and providing his men with much needed cheer. The trip had been hard, tiring and tense, his crew working the job of many men, while keeping Rei and his murderous traitors under tight control. There'd been nothing untoward during the rest of the journey but worry of more trouble had never been far from his mind. They had made it, however, and Carwyn had recovered well from their ordeal. He was a fetching sight with his hair down his back in a single braid and wearing the tunic, long kilt and low soft boots that the prima kailisa had sent for his bride. The orange cloth with gold thread was perfect for him, and despite the garments being what women tended to wear, Carwyn looked adorable. Aleki hoped he could convince his wife to dress that way often.

He turned to shout orders to his pilot to bring the ship into the harbor. Now that they were so close to their destination, he didn't want anything to go wrong. He should have taken the wheel himself, except he felt the need to keep Carwyn close and to present a united front to those of his people watching them come in. Naturally, no one knew about the switch of his bride, and as there was no way to gauge how Carwyn might be received, he didn't want him to face the reception on his own. By the time the ship slid into its slip, a huge crowd had gathered.

No surprise, given the circumstances.

Many of his people would know unimaginable grief from the loss of their relatives from the fighting or the price of betraying their country. He intended to make good on his promise of leniency for those of Rei's men who'd surrendered. That would mean life at hard labor for the prima kailisa instead of death, hardly something their families could take much comfort from. But that was a matter for later. Now, it was all about a triumphant return with the much-needed treaty. From the expressions of the crowd greeting them, many people had already realized that the young man wearing a noblewoman's clothing and plastered to

Aleki's side was the Moorcondian bride they had all come to see.

"Time to disembark, my dear. We must go to court immediately. The prima kailisa will want to meet you and deal with Rei — once she learns of his betrayal."

Carwyn didn't hesitate to go with him, but he put his palm against his stomach. "I'm so nervous. What if she doesn't like me?"

Aleki couldn't help chuckling. "She will, never fear, because she's a discerning woman and you, my dear, are magnificent."

His expression hardened the next moment when Rei was brought up from the hold by Lono and one other man. Dirty and disheveled, he glared with murderous rage at him. The man knew his fate and yet wasn't about to show fear or contrition. If not for the danger the asshole had put Carwyn in, Aleki might have felt some sympathy. Except looking around at the small, exhausted crew who'd brought them home, he remembered the men he'd lost and hardened his heart.

"Bring him."

By the time he and Carwyn had disembarked, the prima kailisa's first minister had arrived to greet them. He disengaged his hold on his wife and bowed. "Minister Mele."

The man did the same. "Kai Aleki." Then turned to face Carwyn and bowed to him as well, although said nothing to indicate he understood who Carwyn was.

Aleki rectified that quickly and loudly so that all around them would hear. "I present my kailisa, Lord Carwyn of Kenworth, cousin to King Auden of Moorcondia. There was a change in the arrangement," he added as if there was nothing remarkable to it.

"Indeed." Like all of his ilk, Mele knew how to pivot quickly in any situation. "Kailisa Aleki, welcome to the Southern Chain." He bowed again.

"Thank you." Carwyn did the same, and there was a noticeable relaxation to his stance.

"I trust the treaty has been signed, kai?"

Pulling the document from his waistband, Aleki presented it. "Yes. Moorcondia is now our official ally."

"Most excellent. Her grace will be pleased." Rei's arrival shifted Mele's attention. "What is this, kai?"

"Perfidy of the highest order." He didn't spare his cousin a glance as he laid out the story of the mutiny for the minister.

The man quivered for a few moments in obvious outrage before gesturing to some of the palace guards who accompanied him. They were there as part of the pomp and circumstance of Aleki's arrival with his foreign bride. Now they had a real job to do. They hauled a sneering Rei off with them. The crowd of onlookers parted for them, even as their murmurs increased over the spectacle.

Mele bowed again. "With your permission, kai, I will precede you and explain matters to the prima kailisa. You and your kailisa should enjoy your triumphant ride through the city. The public is very keen to see you."

"Thank you, minister." With his own bow, Aleki took his wife by his elbow. "Come, my dear. It will give me great pleasure to show you off."

* * * *

Not being anyone of importance his whole life, Carwyn wasn't used to being on display. The carriage ride to the Chainer palace was a slow one. As it wound through the streets of crushed stone, it seemed as if everyone in the entire island had come out to see them. He sat pressed against Aleki's side, trying to smile and not look as intimidated as he felt. His husband's steady presence helped a great deal, but it was still overwhelming. The throngs of people bowed as they passed, then openly stared at him.

"I think some of them are trying to decide if I'm a girl or a boy."

Aleki merely laughed and squeezed his hand. "No one would mistake you for a girl, my dear, even if King Auden and his court were fooled on our wedding day. They see you for what you are."

"Do you think they are upset about me?"

"It is not for them to make such a judgment, but no, I see only acceptance on my people's faces. They want security, and your presence here gives them hope that the Swarm will never touch them. That fact alone endears you to them, but I have no doubt that they will all love you as I do."

Carwyn's heart tripped at that last observation. *Don't be silly. It's only an expression. It doesn't mean he really loves me.* Now was not the time to even feel his husband out about what he'd meant personally. They had arrived at the palace, a sprawling single floor building with open porticos wrapped around it. The outside was a coral-colored stucco. It was the same as what he'd seen throughout the city, although larger and grander than the rest. When the carriage stopped in front, Aleki jumped out of it in a display of strength and glee, then helped Carwyn do the same. As they stood face-to-face for a moment, Aleki surprised him with a quick kiss. The crowd let out a cheer that made Carwyn blush.

He stuck close to his husband's side as they entered the palace and walked down the long, main hall. It was lined with courtiers, and each one quietly bowed as they passed. Like the commoners outside, they openly studied Carwyn, although no one showed any surprise. No doubt word of him had spread ahead of their arrival. He made sure to stand straight and keep his head high. It was important to make a good impression, given that he was a representative of his country. And as a treaty bride, he had the important job of demonstrating that he was prepared to dedicate himself to his husband's people. Still, when they reached a wide archway that led into an open room filled with people, his stomach fluttered with nerves.

"You do me proud, Carwyn...always. Remember that."

With that bit of reassurance, Aleki led him down the open pathway the courtiers left for them. The prima kailisa was visible at the far end. She sat on a beautiful throne decorated by seashells. Around her sat a dozen ladies in lower chairs. Every woman wore elaborate tunics and long kilts, an abundance of rings, bracelets, necklaces and earrings, as well as headdresses from which tiny bells hung. They tinkled musically from the refreshing cross-breeze that permeated the vast open room. Naturally, the prima kailisa's crown was the tallest of them all, as big as her actual head and fanning past her cheek bones. Her stunning dark eyes were heavily made-up, giving her an almost mystical appearance. And while the women's clothing looked light and breezy, the jewelry appeared to weigh them down. Carwyn doubted they did much during the day except perhaps sit almost like statues to be gazed at. None of them smiled as Aleki and Carwyn approached. But as they made their bows at the base of her throne, the woman who ruled over them all gave them a soft expression when she returned the gesture.

"You are full of surprises, Kai Aleki," she said in a warm tone. "Just as you always were as a child."

"There was a minor change in the treaty terms, your grace. Carwyn became my bride with everyone's blessing. He is of the king's blood." The man notably left out the part where Carwyn and Nora had pulled a fast one on all except his husband.

"The treaty has been sealed, so I am pleased with the outcome—however unexpectedly it unfolded." A wave of murmurs behind them caught her attention. "This is a surprise I am not pleased with, however."

Aleki pulled Carwyn to one side as Rei was marched in by two warriors, limping from the stab wound Carwyn had delivered, and forced to kneel in front of his sovereign. The man didn't bow to her, which Carwyn assumed was an insult of the highest order. Carwyn had avoided asking Aleki what the punishment for the treason would be, but he could well imagine. Although a treacherous asshole, Rei managed to show courage in the face of his fate. He stared at the prima kailisa with his head high and his hands clasped behind him.

The prima kailisa said nothing for a long while, staring down at her subject with cool disdain. Finally, she spoke. "Explain yourself, cousin."

"You have no idea what you are dealing with. The Swarm will destroy us all. I was the last hope for our people." The words were spoken without heat, just certainty. They were chilling to hear and elicited low murmurs from the onlookers.

The prima kailisa smacked the arm of her chair, her gold bracelets jingling. "Coward! You acted out of fear and avarice and nothing more, except ambition well above your station. We will defeat the Swarm with the help of our new ally, but you won't be here to witness it." She nodded to someone off to the side.

The biggest warrior Carwyn had ever seen came through the crowd, his short kilt barely containing his thick thighs. His entire torso was covered in complex tattoos. He held a short, thin scabbard cradled in his hands. He placed it on the floor in front of Rei, then stood close to the prima kailisa with his beefy arms folded.

"You know what to do," the woman said to Rei. When the man made no move, she continued. "This way your children will remember you with some honor, and your family will be taken care of. There is no choice, and you must have known what your fate would be if you failed when you started down the path you took."

Again there was silence, and it seemed as if everyone in the throne room held their breath. Although he didn't know for certain, Carwyn thought he understood what was coming. He couldn't help reaching out to clutch his husband's hand. It might show weakness and lack decorum, yet he needed the comfort. Aleki didn't let him down. He took his hand and tugged him in closer.

Finally, Rei reached down and picked up the scabbard. He pulled the long knife out with a slow pull and tossed the scabbard aside. The fine steel flashed in the light as he held it aloft, as if an offering, or maybe he was studying it, making certain of its sharpness. His next movement came suddenly. With a hiss, he twisted the blade and plunged it into his chest. The wet sound and his audible gasp was stomach-turning. It was quick, though. Rei keeled over immediately, his body limp and still. No one said anything or moved a muscle. They simply stared at the traitor's body.

Aleki broke the silence by stepping forward. He tried to release Carwyn's hand, but Carwyn wasn't about to let his husband do anything without him at this point. "Your grace, I also await your judgment."

The woman looked down at him coolly. "Explain yourself."

"I failed you. Rei's treachery should never have gotten as far as it did. My lack of judgment nearly cost you the treaty."

Carwyn didn't like this one bit. His husband had warned him that he might be punished with demotion over the debacle, but this seemed like goading. The prima kailisa hadn't raised the issue, so why was he?

Then the prima kailisa gave a little huff. "I picked Rei to accompany you. By your logic, I should abdicate."

Aleki took another step forward. "Prima kailisa, no. Your people need you. We would accept no other to lead us in these dark times." There was a general murmur of assent throughout the room.

"I quite agree. The matter is closed for both of us." With that, she stood, her ladies with her as if on a silent command and sailed out of the room, the music of their jewelry as an accompaniment. All the courtiers bowed to her.

Aleki dropped Carwyn's hand so that they could do the same. He grabbed it again as soon as they had. "Let us go home, my dear. We must return for the banquet, but there is time for me to show you our home and get some rest."

"That sounds good." He gladly followed his husband away from the violence he'd witnessed and chose to say nothing about his husband's sense of honor in bringing up what he'd considered a failure. The prima kailisa knew her people needed the kai as much as she to survive. Something else did gnaw at him, though. "Will his family really be taken care of? Rei's, I mean."

"Of course. Don't give it another thought. We understand that Rei's wife and children and other family members are not responsible for his acts, although there will be an investigation. If any of the adults were in league with him, they will be expected to do the honorable thing as well. People will talk, as they always do, but they have a decent future to look forward to, nevertheless."

Carwyn felt relief. "That's good. I wasn't sure what would happen and I didn't dare ask."

Aleki pulled him to a stop and cupped his face. "My dear boy, you must always tell me if something bothers you, and you may not have any reason to think so, but my people are civilized. It's the Swarm who are barbarians."

Carwyn dropped gaze. "I'm sorry. I didn't mean to insult you or your people."

"You never could." He lifted Carwyn's chin with one finger and planted a quick kiss on his lips. "Come on. I can't wait to show you our home."

With a lighter heart, Carwyn eagerly went with his husband to greet his new future.

Chapter Ten

Carwyn had always believed that he was a very pampered son of the nobility, but nothing that he'd been privileged to have back home compared to the luxury of being the wife of Kai Aleki. As his husband had shown him around his new home, he couldn't help being dazzled by the large, open rooms, tall windows and abundance of marble in a variety of colors he'd never seen before. And just about everything was swathed in silk, from the furniture to the throw rugs in each room. This also included the opulent canopied bed. He'd been both surprised and delighted to learn that in the Southern Chain, the norm was for married couples to share one bedroom. There would be no nightly visits from his husband. Instead, they would lie down together until morning. He thought the custom was quite practical, given that he hoped to have sex with his husband every day. Except soon they would be parted as the kai set sail to confront the enemy. But he wouldn't think about that just yet.

Perhaps the most enjoyable part of the house was the vast bathing chamber that, while covered, was actually outside and fed by a hot spring. When he'd entered the sunken tub, he'd slid down to his neck with no effort. It was practically a pond, with flower petals scattered over the surface. The scent relaxed him, and the ability to immerse himself in warm fresh water was something he'd missed terribly without realizing it. The enveloping heat also helped to soothe his still-sore muscles. He sighed from the release of it. The only thing missing was his husband. Aleki had business to attend to, and although Carwyn had sensed that he could easily convince the man to stay with him a while longer, he didn't want to be a clingy wife. Grave matters took precedence over his personal pleasure.

"Your pardon, kailisa. Shall I wash your hair now?"

Carwyn opened his eyes to look at the smiling face of the boy who'd been assigned as his body servant. He'd never had a valet who catered to his exclusive care and was used to washing himself. It was just one more thing he would need to get used to in his new home. "Yes, thank you, Kimo." Although it was tempting to stay immersed in the soothing bath, his skin was getting rather wrinkled, and he wanted to primp for when his husband eventually returned.

Kneeling at the edge of the tub behind Carwyn, the boy plucked up his hair and began to work in something sweet-smelling. It was hard not to moan from the amazing feeling of those clever fingers rubbing his scalp. It was more luxury, this pampering, not merely tending to a necessary chore. He appreciated how Kimo was making an effort to give him pleasure and succeeding. The experience didn't end there, either. Once Kimo was done with Carwyn's hair, he helped him out of the tub and toweled him dry from head to toe with vigorous rubbing.

"Come, kailisa. Now I will give you a massage." The boy gestured to a high bench that was covered with a silk quilt.

"Oh." Carwyn gnawed at his lower lip. This wasn't something he was familiar with. "I'm not really hurt anywhere that needs tending…" His muscles were loose after the bath.

Kimo flashed him a smile. "Not to worry, your grace. This is for making you feel good—relaxed. Besides, the kai left very specific instructions on this matter."

"I don't think it's possible for me to be more so after that bath."

Kimo giggled but continued to silently insist that Carwyn succumb to his ministrations. Not wanting to offend or get the boy in trouble with Aleki—and intrigued anyway—he went to lie down, face up on the bench. It was pillowy soft. "Like this?"

"Yes, kailisa. We'll start with your front, then move onto your back. I am very good. You'll see."

Kimo was as true to his word. When he took one of Carwyn's feet in his hands, slippery from some kind of scented oil, the sensation was amazing. He'd never experienced someone working his muscles except to aid in the recovery of an injury. That had always been more about pain than pleasure. This was purely a comforting touch, especially as his feet had recovered from the harshness of running around the island he'd escaped to with Aleki. All that life-threatening drama seemed so long ago. He gladly relegated it to the past and simply immersed himself in the sensation of his body being kneaded. To his mortification, however, as

Kimo worked up to Carwyn's calves, then thighs, his body misinterpreted the attention before he could stop it.

His eyes popped open. "I'm sorry! That's entirely unintentional."

Kimo giggled again. "Not to worry, your grace. It always happens and is a sign that I am pleasing you."

Alarm shot through him, chasing away all the boy's hard work. "I don't want that! Not from anyone other than my husband."

Kimo removed his hands from Carwyn's thigh and stepped up to the end of the bench where his head was. "Of course not, your grace. That is a part of you only the kai may touch. Please, close your eyes and allow me to relax you." He placed both hands on Carwyn's shoulders and did something magical with his thumbs.

"O-okay." Carwyn couldn't have kept his eyes open if he'd tried. So he once more gave into the sensation of being pampered. He started to drift off, then returned to alertness when there was a change in his massage. From one moment to the next, Kimo's hands morphed, became larger, stronger. Carwyn couldn't keep the smile off his face. "I think I'd like you to return to my lower half now."

"As you wish, kailisa."

The mere sound of Aleki's deep voice sent a shiver through Carwyn. His breath hitched as the man clasped his hips and started pressing his thumbs into his groin. He moaned loudly, sure that they must be alone and not really caring one way or the other. His husband could play with his body however he desired, and Carwyn wanted him to know the effect he had on him. His cock hardened to a painful state, and his balls ached with the need to be touched. But Aleki didn't move on to those places. He kept working the muscles all around them. On another groan, Carwyn bucked his hips in a silent command.

Aleki chuckled. "So impatient, my wife."

"Please." He didn't care how needy he was being.

"Very well. But only because I'm sure I can make you come again when it suits me." That was all Aleki said before he clasped Carwyn's dick with a firm grip and jerked him with fast, sure strokes that ended with his thumb swiping over Carwyn's cockhead.

Carwyn groaned and writhed, kept in place by that hold on his shaft and the press of Aleki's other hand on his hip. He wanted to make the experience last, loving the way his husband worked his dick. It proved impossible. With a cry, he arched his back and came all over his husband's hand. Drops of warm cum splashed onto his chest, but that hardly mattered. There was a tub right there for them to clean up in and perhaps continue to enjoy each other in other ways. That nascent plan died moments later when Aleki wiped him clean with a soft cloth, then helped him roll over.

"Time for your back," Aleki whispered into Carwyn's ear, his warm breath both tickling and provocative.

With his cock mashed between his body and the bench, there wasn't much room for it to do anything other than recover. The same was true for every part of his body. He lay limp, absorbing his husband's firm kneading of every inch of the back of him. When the man reached Carwyn's ass, however, he felt a renewed sense of arousal. Aleki clasped both butt cheeks with his big hands and squeezed while he slid his thumbs between them. Carwyn's hole clenched at the unspoken promise.

Aleki removed his hands, but before Carwyn could voice disapproval, oil dribbled down his crack. A wide thumb followed it and slid easily through the puckered ring. He welcomed it and moaned his approval as it twisted and thrust to open him up. Two fingers invaded him next, turning to rub his prostate. He would have levitated off the bench but for Aleki holding him in place with his palm pressed against the small of his back. Carwyn wiggled and shuddered in response to the delightful assault. His entrapment added to the pleasure, ramping it up, making his cock fill with blood, even though it had nowhere to go. He found himself pleading breathlessly, his hands clenching rhythmically on either side of his head with the thrusting.

Finally, Aleki pulled out his fingers and climbed onto the bench. He lay over Carwyn, holding himself up with his elbows pressed against Carwyn's side. The man's massive cock slid up and down the crack before settling against his hole. With one push, it impaled him, balls deep. He shuddered and cried out, coming once again merely from being filled by dick and despite the lack of freedom his own cock had. It didn't matter. His husband could bring him to climax any time with little effort. He was that primed for the man—always.

Aleki took his time, thrusting with long, slow strokes, whispering provocative words into his ear. Most of it was a jumble of nonsense but one word was clear. "Mine." Then, "You belong to me." His husband didn't try to soften his possessiveness.

"Y-yes." No response had been demanded, yet Carwyn gave one anyway because it was true. He did belong to this man. *I love you.* He wanted to shout those words out loud. They stuck in his throat, because he still feared it was too soon to declare his feelings. Theirs was a political marriage, and it was enough at the moment that his husband wanted him, claimed him with a strength demonstrating how much.

With a final surge, Aleki yelled his release, his warm cum spurting inside Carwyn's ass, coating his channel, marking him. His husband collapsed on top of him, his weight pressing him down. The large man's shudders reverberated through Carwyn, too. There was a kind of power here, to be able to render a strong man limp, a blanket of lax muscles and heavy breath. Too soon, Aleki pushed up and off both Carwyn and the bench. Clasping one of Carwyn's hands, he said, "Come, my dear. I believe you're in need of a second bath."

Carwyn opened one eye. "Does that mean I get another massage?"

"Still a greedy boy." His husband swatted his ass playfully and with little sting.

Hmm. Yes, that spanking thing definitely has possibilities. For the moment, rolling around in warm water would have to do. He let Aleki pull him to his feet.

* * * *

"Is this all right?"

Carwyn peered at his reflection in the mirror. His wife had been sitting quietly at his dressing table as Kimo had primped him for the banquet. The servant was proving up to the challenge thrust upon him by the housekeeper when it became known that the kailisa was a man, not a woman. And because Kimo was also a distant relative and someone close to Carwyn's age, Aleki hoped he'd be a good companion to his wife while he was away. The thought of leaving made him sad now, whereas before he'd been eager to confront the Swarm in their own waters. Then he'd expected his new wife would hold no interest to him other than what she brought to the treaty. His situation had changed. Carwyn was more than a temptation in his bed. He had infiltrated Aleki's heart and taken residence there. It was an unexpected development but not unwanted. It seemed too soon in their relationship to voice those kinds of feelings. He was sensitive to the fact that, while Carwyn obviously enjoyed being wedded to a man, he'd only married him to save his cousin Nora from a fate she'd found repellent. That wasn't the best foundation to form a loving bond, and he didn't want Carwyn to feel pressured to respond in kind whether he loved him or not. Aleki could at least make his wife as happy as possible.

He smiled into the mirror. "You are exquisite, my dear."

Carwyn gave him a shy smile in return, then tossed his head. "The bells in my hair are okay? I mean, I figure it's mostly a woman's style."

"Yes, but threading them through braids instead of wearing a headdress is something young men do occasionally, especially on such a formal and happy occasion. The prima kailisa and her ladies will find you adorable."

Carwyn stood and turned to face him. Kimo had dressed him in a tunic with belled sleeves and a long kilt, both in burnt orange silk with blue and yellow thread making a design of flowers and birds. Gold sandals adorned his feet. It was one of the many outfits his family had made sure would greet his new wife upon her arrival. Nevertheless, they'd been adapted to

Carwyn's male form in quick order, and while feminine, highlighted his delicate masculine beauty. Just looking at his wife made him nearly hard again, but he'd taken Carwyn a few times already that afternoon. He didn't want the boy to become sore, nor did they have the time for such sport. Besides, at the end of the evening, he'd have his wife in his bed and in his arms again.

"Come." Taking Carwyn by the hand, he led him out of the house and into the open carriage for the short ride to the palace. It was a glorious evening, warm yet not humid. Unlike earlier as they'd hurried to present themselves in court, this ride allowed him to appreciate the simple pleasure of having Carwyn by his side and pointing out his country's features to someone who'd never experienced them before.

The Moorcondian boy was open with his curiosity. "Everything is so colorful. And it's as if your city lives inside the jungle. There's so much to explore and learn." He smiled at him. "I want to become a good Chainer, so you'll have to teach me about my new life in order to keep me from embarrassing you."

Aleki brought his wife's hand to his lips for a kiss. "You could never do that, and it was easy to see that despite your upbringing in the country, you are a natural denizen of a court. Ours is not much different than yours. Continue to be your sweet, charming self and all will come to adore you as I do."

Carwyn rolled his eyes. "Thank you, husband, but you see me with your dick as much as your eyes. I promise to represent you in court as best I know how with my tongue instead of my body—which belongs to you and no one else," he added with seriousness.

Aleki frowned, not liking that his wife saw his worth merely in his ability to bring him pleasure. "Your fidelity is not in question, my dear. My only concern is that I have to abandon you in a foreign place. Even with my mother and sisters arriving soon for a visit, they will be strangers to you, however kind I know they will be."

"I look forward to getting to know them, and this is home now. I don't want to talk about your leaving, either." His hand spasmed in Aleki's grip, and he looked away.

Sorry to remind his wife that he would be without him in a short amount of time, Aleki jumped to change the subject. "The feast tonight will rival the ones your king honored me with. I can't wait to introduce you to our cuisine, and there will be fireworks later."

That caught Carwyn's attention. He smiled broadly. "Really? I've rarely seen them."

"They originated here, I'm proud to say. There will be beautiful colors...and loud explosions."

Leaning into him, Carwyn said, "That's okay. I'll have you by my side, so the noise won't bother me. You always keep me safe."

Pleased with the vote of confidence while knowing that wasn't entirely true, Aleki put aside his darker thoughts and gathered his wife in his arms. Tonight was for fun. Work would come soon enough.

* * * *

The reality of duty showed up earlier than Aleki expected. As the last of the fireworks burst in the sky above the harbor, the alarm bell for an approaching ship rang out. Everyone dropped their gaze to the water. The shadow of many ships heading their way came into view.

"Who's coming?" There was worry in Carwyn's voice.

Aleki answered quickly to allay his wife's fears. "Those are your ships, my dear."

"Mine?"

"Moorcondian ones."

"Really? I thought they'd be a few days behind us in arriving."

"They would have been if Rei hadn't diverted us."

"Oh. Of course." Carwyn's tone was dejected.

Understanding why his wife was saddened by the news, Aleki moved to soothe his thoughts. "No one will leave just yet. The Moorcondian ships need to re-supply, and detailed plans of attack have to be made. That will take some time. We have to be careful in our next moves. Let's go down to the docks and greet them. I'm sure your people will be gratified to see you."

"I suppose." Biddable boy that he was, Carwyn didn't drag his feet or plead tiredness. Instead, he hurried along to their carriage, then stood at his side as the ships came sailing in.

The first one surprised him. It was clearly a fighting ship, yet more of a clipper and not big enough for the kind needed to lead a battle on the seas. The sight would have alarmed him that their new allies were either not equipped to help as much as they thought or not truly interested in doing so. Using the Southern Chain as a sacrifice against the Swarm to weaken them could possibly be their strategy. But no, right behind that ship came the real Moorcondian navy, massive frigates primed for war came over the horizon. His worry evaporated, although curiosity remained. What purpose did the smaller ship serve?

Carwyn grabbed his arm with both hands and practically bounced on his toes. "It's the Intrepid! My brother's ship."

"The cartographer?"

"Yes. I had no idea he was coming here, too."

"Neither did I." Given Carwyn's enthusiasm, he was glad that this scout was joining the rest of the fleet. There would be a few days for him to visit with his brother. It would make Aleki's own preparations easier if his wife was occupied.

They watched the Intrepid pull up to the slip with mounting excitement. At least Carwyn was practically vibrating with it, the tinkling of his hair decorations giving him away. When the gangplank was lowered, Aleki moved down the dock to meet the guests halfway. As the prima kailisa's chief warrior, it was his duty to bid the Moorcondians welcome. A barrel of a man came onshore first, the captain obviously, even without all the brass and braiding of his uniform. Aleki understood that it was the Moorcondian equivalent of tattoos, marking rank and commanding respect. Two less impressive men followed him and a boy wearing civilian clothing and with a large satchel slung over his shoulder came after them. He looked so much like Carwyn that Aleki knew a jolt of familiarity and a stirring in his loins before getting himself under control.

The captain stopped in front of him and made a decent bow. "Kai Aleki, I presume. I am Captain Ambrose and honored for you to greet me."

Aleki let go of his wife to make a bow of his own. Carwyn did as well, without prompting, but his attention remained fixed on his brother. "Welcome to the Southern Chain, Captain Ambrose. This is my kailisa, Lord Carwyn of Kenworth."

The man's gaze slid to Carwyn. A hungry look passed over his eyes before he banked it. "My pleasure. We encountered the other ships in the fleet on their way here. I was glad to learn that the treaty had been signed, as my men and I are eager to travel farther into Swarm waters to chart them. Having his majesty's war ships at our back is a welcome development. I had expected to meet with Princess Eleanora, of course." His expression read annoyed.

"A happy change in circumstances," Aleki responded with cheer and just a hint of warning. He wouldn't allow this man to denigrate his wife.

"Certainly." Ambrose gestured toward the two officers and introduced them. Then, he added, "And I expect you already know about Lord Cariad."

Before Aleki could reply, Carwyn bolted from his side, past the navy men, and ran right into his brother's arms. The other boy was close enough for a better look, and while he and Carwyn were obviously brothers with the same coloring, height and build, there were clear differences, too. Where Carwyn was naturally carefree with a ready smile, Lord Cariad bore a serious expression. Even while hugging his brother, the boy looked wary. Aleki supposed that a long journey in dangerous waters could do that to anyone. It hardly mattered, in any event, because Carwyn was so happy. That's all that was important to him.

Aleki looked around and spotted Mele hurrying to his side. *Good.* This was now a political moment. Someone needed to take charge of the official welcome and presentations to the prima kailisa for Ambrose and the captains of the other ships arriving. It would take most if not all the night for them to make port. It was his duty to remain, but his wife needn't. The boys huddled together, speaking in low tones, likely catching up. He wasn't sure how long it had been since they'd seen each other. Giving them some private time for their reunion was the right thing to do.

"My dear wife." It pleased him when Carwyn immediately raised his head and turned his face toward him. "Take your brother to our home. Kimo will help you settle him in the guest quarters."

With his arm looped around Cariad's, Carwyn sauntered back to him, the bells in his hair ringing softly. "Are you sure, Aleki? My duty is by your side," he added in a soft voice.

The simple statement pleased him, and he did love having the boy with him. But he was tired and no doubt wanted time with his brother. "I prefer knowing you are tucked into my bed and getting your well-earned sleep. Take the carriage," he added with a gesture toward the street.

Carwyn looked torn but acquiesced without a murmur of dissent. "Very well. Come on, Cariad. Wait 'til you see what counts as a bathtub here." He started forward but his brother stayed put.

Cariad flicked his gaze at Ambrose. "By your leave, Captain?"

"You are only under my command while onboard ship, my lord. The kai is in charge here, and he wants you to go, so go."

There was an underlying tone in those brusque words that he didn't like. He made a mental note to ask his wife later on what his brother had to say about his stay on the Intrepid. The work they were doing was too important for any conflict among the crew, not even if it came from the captain.

The brothers didn't need urging, Carwyn joyfully tugging Cariad along, the latter boy hitching the bag he carried higher on his shoulder. He looked tired, too. Aleki was glad to have forced the issue. Once they were on their way, he focused back to where the captain and Mele spoke in earnest about provisions. The tedium of the administrative matters would send him into a stupor, but the shadows of large sails of several ships against the moonlight lifted his spirits. This was what he'd gone to accomplish when he'd ventured to Moorcondia. The alliance gave them a real chance to defeat the Swarm. And, although it wasn't important in the larger scheme of things, he had obtained the perfect wife for him. It was going to be torture to leave the boy, but there was no hope for it.

* * * *

Carwyn watched as his brother roamed the large guest room Kimo had escorted them to, touching the carved wood of the furniture and sliding his palm across the silk fabric. "I know... It's opulent, right? I always thought we lived a privileged life, then I went to King Auden's palace and realized we lived a backwater existence. This, though..."

Cariad sat on the high, soft bed and bounced. "Everything is so exotic here. Nothing is like back home, not the plants or animals or buildings. I've been looking forward to docking here ever since the captain said we were on our way to reprovision and see about the status of the treaty." He gave Carwyn a pointed look. "I didn't expect to find you. Nora has talked you into something—again."

Tamping down a spike of annoyance, Carwyn went to join him. "She did no such thing." He threw himself on his back and stared up at the draping blue silk canopy above the bed. "If you must know, it was the dowager queen's idea that I take her place."

Cariad lay down beside him. "Interesting. Tell me the whole story." Once Carwyn had, his brother remained silent for a short while. "You've left something out."

"What?"

Cariad turned his head to look at him. "How do you feel about all of this?"

"Oh." Carwyn laughed. "You've seen my husband. How do you think I feel?"

"Hmm. He is impressive and just your type, if memory serves. You've always pined after the big strong ones."

"As opposed to...honestly, I don't know what kind of man appeals to you."

"I'm not interested in men." It was the same answer Cariad always gave. "Or women, either," he added quite unnecessarily. "But I am concerned with our country's safety, and this treaty is paramount to defeating the Swarm. That doesn't mean I want you to be sacrificed unnecessarily for it."

"I'm happy. Please believe me. Being Aleki's wife is going to take some getting used to because I don't yet know his culture very well. And I've yet to meet his mother and sisters. They'll be arriving soon and probably after he leaves. Thinking about that makes me a little queasy because I want them to like me, naturally. I have no doubts about my and Aleki's personal relationship, though. We get along quite well, and he's magnificent in bed," he couldn't help adding.

Cariad snorted. "No surprise there. He doesn't wear a lot of clothing."

"It's warm here. The men usually wear only a short kilt."

"Yours is nearly to your ankles, and no one's catching an eyeful of your chest." He reached over to flick one of the bells in Carwyn's braid. "I didn't see any jewelry woven into his hair, either."

Carwyn shrugged. "I'm dressed more like a woman here."

"Does that make you happy?"

"It doesn't make me unhappy. Unlike when I put on Nora's wedding gown, these clothes are unfamiliar to me, so they don't trigger any automatic rejection in my mind. And…I like looking pretty for my husband. Oh gods," he added, suddenly unable to keep his feelings to himself. "I've fallen in love with him."

Cariad rolled onto his side to face him. "Seriously? You barely know him."

"Tell me the obvious. It's beyond ridiculous."

"But, you do?"

"I do." He rolled over as well to look Cariad eye-to-eye. "I think I started to fall in love with him the moment I first saw him standing in the throne room, magnificent in his kilt and tattoos. He's the fantasy man I never knew about. How could I ever dream up such a vision?"

"Does he know how you feel?"

Carwyn couldn't hold back the gasp. "No! He has too many responsibilities as it is. He doesn't need to deal with his wife's clingy emotions. And with his leaving so soon, I won't have a chance to ease him into it. I hate the fact that he has to go off to war while I sit here being pampered. He should have me by his side. We made a good team when his men mutinied."

"Whoa." Cariad sat up. "What?"

"Oh yeah. I forgot. You don't know the story."

Cariad started pulling off his boots. "Tell me, and let's get comfortable while you do so."

It was like being back at home as children, as they snuggled next to each other and Carwyn told the tale of his adventure at sea. He made his husband the hero, naturally, because without Aleki's training and skill, they never would have made it. "It was terrifying," he admitted. "And exciting at the same time."

"Well, I'm glad you think so. It sounds positively dreadful. I live in fear of being caught in a battle — or simply just caught. Who knows what kind of hideous fate would be visited on me by the Swarm. You're lucky to be left behind in the relative safety of this place."

"You say that, but you volunteered to go. That took great courage, Cariad."

His brother shrugged. "It's the work that I'm interested in. Talk about excitement. There are so many islands out there, and I'm the first to make maps of them. People will use them for generations to come — my own contribution to the greater good. I just have to survive being out to sea for the gods know how long."

Carwyn wrinkled his nose. "It sounds deadly dull to me, except for the part where you're putting yourself in danger. What's up with that Captain Ambrose, by the way?"

"Oh, you caught that, did you?" Cariad sighed. "He keeps trying to get me into his bed."

"Eew! He's old and ugly."

"And *married*. He says what a man does while out at sea is his own business, not his wife's. Even if I were interested in men in general and him in particular, I still wouldn't subscribe to that notion."

"Do you want me to see if Aleki can scare him into leaving you alone?" He didn't like the idea of his brother being trapped on a ship with someone pressuring him like that.

"No. It's fine. He's like an annoying bug, and the rest of the crew steer clear of me because they think I'm already his boy." He yawned loudly. "All this heat makes me tired."

Carwyn patted his arm. "Go to sleep then."

"Will you stay with me until I do?"

"Of course. That's what brothers are for."

Chapter Eleven

Aleki was irked when he found his bed empty. The settling of the Moorcondian ships had taken the better part of the night. With the sun rising, he hoped for a few hours of sleep before meeting with the captains and his own council to plan their move against the Swarm. But a cold bed didn't appeal to him, so he went looking for Carwyn, finding him in the most obvious place. He couldn't help but smile at the sight of his wife and his brother sprawled together in the bed. No doubt they'd fallen asleep catching up with each other's lives. It was good that Carwyn had someone to talk to. He would make friends here eventually, but this brief interlude with someone who already knew and who loved him would help alleviate his own guilt at having to spend so much time away from him.

I'm stupid in love with the boy. He would find the right moment to confess his feelings before setting off. There was no guarantee that he would return, and he wanted Carwyn to know for a certainty that their marriage meant more to him than a treaty. He carefully lifted his wife in his arms, enjoying the way he curled into him. *So trusting*. When he laid him down on their marital bed, Carwyn stirred a little but didn't fully wake. As soon as Aleki slid in next to him, the boy snuggled against his side, sighed, then dropped back into sleep. Aleki followed him, content as any man anywhere.

* * * *

His training allowed him to wake after a short rest. The sun was shining through the sheer curtains of his window. He knew he should get up yet couldn't quite let go of the warm bundle pressed against him. His cock was already awake, and even as he chided himself to have more control, his wife crawled onto him.

"Fuck me."

The command, given in a soft and sleepy voice, made Aleki smile. He reversed their positions and reached for the pot on the low table by the bed. This convenience was one of his first orders to his own body servant when he'd arrived home. He made short work of slicking his dick, and his slippery finger found a warm welcome by Carwyn's hole. Aleki slid into it with no resistance. He thrusted slowly, pushing one of Carwyn's legs to give him better access. For the first time since their wedding night, he wanted to take his time, draw out the pleasure for them both. But the feel of warm cum splashing against his chest and the clenching of Carwyn's hole snapped his control. He came with a low groan, mashing his pelvis against his wife's until he wrung himself dry. Still, he wanted to simply lie there, joined and sated. It was a moment of pure peace and one of the memories he'd take out to sea with him.

"I will think of you often while I'm out there. You will become my port of call once this terrible business is over." He rolled onto his back so as not to crush his wife, keeping him in his embrace, nevertheless.

Carwyn ran his fingers lightly over Aleki's chest, a soothing, affectionate gesture. "We don't have to be parted," he said in a near whisper.

Aleki frowned. "What?"

Carwyn pushed up to rest his chin on his fist and stared at him earnestly. "I can come with you. We'll fight together the way we did against Rei."

Aleki was rarely at a loss for words. He gazed into his wife's eyes, saw that he was serious, then shook his head. "No."

"No?" Carwyn sat up now. "What do you mean by that?"

"My dear. 'No' is one of the easiest words to understand. You will *not* come with me. Instead, you will stay here, as safe as anyone can be in the Southern Chain."

"But, Aleki, I'm not like other civilians, because I'm trained in warfare. You know that and have seen my skill for yourself. I simply need to be taught some basics about sailing on a large ship so that I can be of use as one of the crew. I've given this a lot of thought and talking to Cariad about his experiences onboard the Intrepid has convinced me this is the right course. He's risking his life for the sake of both our peoples and anyone else the Swarm might menace. I want to do my part in that as well. Sitting around here and gossiping with your female relatives, however charming they may be, hardly counts as that."

Aleki rose to a sitting position himself, dumbfounded by the conversation. This was not something he'd anticipated, but he damn well knew how it was going to end. "The answer is no, Carwyn. You were magnificent when we needed to survive the mutiny. It was unexpected, and you handled yourself very well. I've praised you mightily about it and will continue to do so for the rest of my life. That doesn't mean you are a warrior or that I'd ever deliberately lead you into danger."

He got out of bed and grabbed the kilt he'd tossed on the floor earlier. "I don't have time for this nonsense. I have meetings to attend to. Go have breakfast with your brother, then have Kimo show you around the city. You both deserve to have an enjoyable day." He turned to leave. A quick bath was in order.

Carwyn thumped his hand on the bed before shoving to his feet. "Aleki, we are *not* done discussing this."

He paused, then closed his eyes for a moment, before looking at his wife over his shoulder. "My dear, this is not a discussion. I'm telling you that you are *not* coming with me. I am Kai Aleki, commander of the prima kailisa's fleet and your husband. I decide who sails with me and what is necessary for your well-being. My word on this is final."

He didn't miss the squeal of outrage, nor the thump of something hitting the doorway behind him. It was tempting to return to the bedroom and demonstrate to his wife just how much he controlled matters. A good fucking would help ease the tension. But he didn't have the time and no doubt Carwyn would be too incensed to be wooed onto his back. Better to give it time. Smart boy that he was, his wife would see the wisdom in his decision—eventually.

* * * *

"The plan is a good one, kai."

Aleki gave the minister the side-eye. "When it's the only one available, it better be good." It didn't take being a strategy genius to realize that they had to slowly make their way to where the Swarm seemed to generate from, clearing each island as they went. The alternative was to simply head full speed into the enemy's waters and risk being surrounded if they'd set up outposts along the way. "How sure are we of the accuracy of the maps provided by Captain Ambrose?"

"As much as we can be. Our cartographers are impressed with what Lord Cariad has done. When they match it up to what we already have, it's a perfect fit, and we've been at it for generations. He's young but seems to have some uncanny ability to see the ocean and the landmasses as if he hovered above it all like a bird. We are making multiple copies so that each ship will have what there is. Captain Ambrose will set sail to continue his mission as soon as we're done."

That was as much a pity as it was necessary, because it would give Carwyn too little time with his brother. That thought led to his reliving the squabble from the morning, something he'd put out of his mind during the council meeting. Maybe a shorter visit with Cariad was a good thing, given that he'd put notions in Carwyn's head that were outrageously inappropriate, whether the boy had intended to or not. The memory of the fight had him fuming all over again. He wasn't used to being challenged by those under his command. And perhaps that was the real problem — Carwyn was his wife, not one of his warriors, however much the boy wished to be.

"Check on their progress, minister. I have some personal matters to attend to."

With mutual bows, they split up. Aleki chose to walk home, needing the exercise to cool his blood and form another plan, one where he expressed himself more clearly and logically so that he and Carwyn wouldn't be at odds for the few days they had left together. Leaving him would be hard, but knowing he was as safe as possible would allow him to focus only on the fight ahead. And his mother and sisters were undoubtedly already on their way from their home island to greet the new family member. They would provide his wife with company. He was certain they would love the boy as well.

He headed straight to their bedroom when he arrived home, displeased but not surprised to find it empty. Fight or not, his wife was hardly going to laze about in bed, waiting for his return. The boy was too industrious to pamper himself. Aleki could only hope that he wasn't out and about in the city. He hunted up the housekeeper, who told him where to find his wife, relieved that he was still home. It surprised him, although it probably shouldn't, that Carwyn was in the small, convenient training ground that Aleki kept to hone his skills. He heard the thwack of an arrow hitting its mark before he located his wife in the archery range. As he rounded the hedge corner, Carwyn let another one fly. It hit very close to the previous effort, which was dead center.

"You are indeed an excellent shot."

His wife looked over his shoulder with a disdainful expression. "You shouldn't be so surprised. You've seen for yourself how accurate I am. That skill saved both our lives," he added quite unnecessarily as that moment on the ship when his wife had killed the sentry was indelibly etched on his mind. Instead of notching another arrow, Carwyn put the bow down and drank from a jug. Water slid off his chin and down his bare chest. The boy wore only a short kilt and as fetching as it was to have so much creamy skin on display, the sun was still relatively high.

Aleki took a few steps closer. "You should have a tunic on, so you won't burn. We aren't as exposed as we were on the ship, but the tree cover only protects so much. It will take time for your skin to adapt to our sun, if it ever does."

Carwyn scowled. "Oh, give it a rest, Aleki." There was a bite to his tone, not hurt or petulant, *angry.* "You can't protect me everywhere, all the time from everything."

I have to try. "You'll have to forgive me worrying about you so much." His own voice had an edge to it that he hadn't intended. "That's what a good husband does. My father taught me as much." And he wished the man were still alive so that he could seek his advice. He didn't know how to handle having a man as a wife. The rules that he would have applied to a woman didn't work quite so well. As formidable as Princess Eleanora had seemed, he doubted she would have demanded to sail into battle with him.

Carwyn eyed him over the rim of the jug and there appeared to be a softening in his gaze. "Kimo slathered some kind of cream all over me to block out the effects of the sun." He put the water down and held up a pot. "I brought it outside with me to reapply as he recommended. Then he stood with hands on his hips and a glare in his eyes. "I'm not stupid," he added with a sulk that was more familiar.

Aleki felt on firmer ground. "When have I ever given the impression I thought you were?" He took a step forward. "My dear, all I want is what's best for you."

"Which *you* get to decide on."

"Not always, but in this, yes. Carwyn, you must know that coming with me would be a disaster. If nothing else, I will worry too much where you are and if you're safe. You'd be a distraction that I can't afford. It would put the rest of my warriors...and me, at risk." He hated admitting his own vulnerabilities, but Carwyn had already seen that for himself. No one was invincible.

It was the right thing to say, however. His wife's shoulders slumped, and he stared at the ground. "I don't want to endanger you or your men. It's only that I'll worry terribly back here, not knowing what's happening to you."

"Oh, my dear." Spreading his arms wide, he moved to embrace his wife. Carwyn stepped back and while the rejection stung, Aleki respected the unspoken demand. He dropped his arms and stopped. "You know I will do everything I can to succeed, and if the worst happens, my family will take care of you. And you can return to Moorcondia without harming the treaty."

Carwyn shot him a look of fury. "You think that's what I'm worried about, that I'll be stuck here without you to keep me happy for the rest of my life?"

"Well, I..." He'd assumed. Why wouldn't he?

"You idiot!" His wife practically screamed the insult and his hands hung in fists. "I'm terrified of losing you. *You*. Not my freedom or even my way of life. I want to go and be by your side because I love you."

Stunned, Aleki froze on the outside while his insides hummed with sudden joy. His heartbeat sped up, his stomach did a very unmanly flip-flop and his dick hardened. "You do?" was all he managed to say.

"Of course I do." Carwyn threw up his hands. "Why else am I here? I dressed myself up as a woman and risked the king's wrath and the treaty by pretending to be Nora. I did all of that not because the dowager queen ordered me to or out of loyalty to my cousin. I did it because I fell in love with you from the moment you came striding into the throne room. I'm that pathetic," he concluded with an audible sniff and blinking back tears.

"My dear wife." Aleki closed the gap between them and grabbed Carwyn in a tight hug before he could evade him.

At first the boy struggled to free himself, then stiffened and finally collapsed against Aleki and wept on his chest. It was a cascade of tears and trembling that shook Carwyn's entire body, no doubt having built up over their journey. All the fear and fighting for their lives had finally caught up with Carwyn. He hadn't shed a single tear, no matter how grave their situation had become, holding back his fear, being stoic. Aleki was simply glad to be there for him, although he was also the catalyst for the dam bursting. No matter, he would do his best to fix what he'd broken.

Comfort turned quickly into something else as the crying eased, and Carwyn wrapped his arms tightly around him. They were both erect now, something that their kilts couldn't hide. He would have tried to shift his position to make his arousal less obvious, but when he tried, Carwyn held him in place. Then grabbing his topknot, the boy pulled his head down as he lifted his own up. Their lips met and their control snapped at the same time. It wasn't clear who tugged whom to the ground, and it hardly mattered. Aleki ended up on his back, and before he realized what his wife was doing, his kilt was open and his dick standing up proud.

He reached for Carwyn and came up empty. The boy evaded his grasp but only to fetch the pot of cream. He straddled Aleki without a hitch, equally naked and hard. Aleki clasped the slender shaft and tugged it, eliciting a groan that caused his own cock to jump. When he tried to grab his wife by his hips to roll him over, the boy slapped at him. His intent became obvious as he dug out fingers full of cream and reached behind to minister to his own hole. The spit in Aleki's mouth dried, and he could do no more than lie there and watch.

With a determined look in his eyes, Carwyn positioned himself over Aleki's cock, put it in place and sat on it in one swift move. They both cried out with arched backs, and it was torturous to keep himself from coming. His dick was encased in the tight, warm channel of his wife's ass, and the way that hole clenched around him... No, he had to hold out and let Carwyn take charge. The boy needed this, and Aleki was hardly in a position to complain, given the exquisite pleasure his wife was showering him with. Placing both palms on Aleki's chest, Carwyn pushed up until the head of Aleki's cock nearly popped out of the boy's hole. Then he lowered himself once more, slowly and with his gaze fixed on him. They stared into each other's eyes as Carwyn repeated the process, his steady movements driving Aleki mad. And apparently his wife was losing control as well, because it all changed in an instant, the boy riding him with a quick, steady rhythm that made it hard for Aleki to keep his eyes open. He had to, though. Watching his wife as he claimed his cock with an impressive mastery was too wonderful to miss. And when the boy's dick released its cum, Aleki allowed himself to finally let go.

* * * *

The thumping of Aleki's heart echoed into Carwyn's ear as he pressed his face against the man's chest. The beat had slowed, as had his own, but neither of them had moved since he'd collapsed onto his husband. The tip of the man's cock was still inside him. He loved the feel of it, the physical connection that was more primal than any hug or kiss could ever be. *Maybe if we stay like this, he won't leave me.* It was a silly thought. Aleki would set sail and soon. And he would do so knowing that Carwyn loved him. What the man would do with such knowledge was impossible to say. At least he hadn't laughed in his face and called him a silly boy when he'd confessed his feelings.

Aleki rubbed his hand up and down Carwyn's back. "Are you all right?"

"Of course. I've gotten used to taking your cock. It felt amazing."

"I'm glad to hear that but it's not what I meant. How do you feel, emotionally?"

Carwyn sighed. "Fine. Embarrassed," he admitted.

"Why?"

"Because I shouldn't have kicked up such a fuss about going with you. And there's that whole 'I love you' part, a burden that you don't need right now."

Aleki reversed their positions without warning. He stared down at him, a look of concern on his face. "You think my hearing that was a bad thing?" Before Carwyn could answer, the infuriating man threw back his head and laughed.

Carwyn slapped his chest. "It's not funny."

Aleki's sobered. "No, it's not. Delightful. Fantastic. Amazing. Those are better words to describe what you confessed."

"I don't understand." He couldn't allow himself to even speculate. If he got it wrong, the disappointment would be crushing.

Aleki kissed him sweetly. "Yes, you do. I went to Moorcondia thinking I was doing my duty, nothing more. I was determined to make the best of it, help save my people and maybe try to extricate both the princess and me from what could only be a loveless marriage once the Swarm was dealt with. Then you came walking toward me, all covered in creamy lace, and I knew that my fate had changed for the better. Now, I know that it changed for the very best. I love you, Carwyn." He fingered the marriage bracelet. "I put this on as a symbol of my fidelity, more out of custom than anything else. Seeing it every day on you gives me comfort. It's as if a part of me is always touching you. My wife," he whispered before kissing him again.

Tears threatened to overwhelm him. He beat them back. While he hadn't dared hope to hear these words, there was no doubt in his husband's voice. And Aleki needed him to be strong. "Saying goodbye to you will be the hardest thing I've ever done. I will, though. That's a promise. No more talk of my coming with you. Let's just make the most of the time we have left."

"My sweet wife, you and I were born to privilege and with that, we owe our people a large measure of duty. Leaving you will be unbearable for me, too. It's for the greater good, though. Knowing that is what will allow me to leave. Having you to come home to will be the extra inspiration I have to fight fiercely, win and return safely."

"If loving me gives you more incentive to protect yourself, then I'm glad. But what will I do while you're gone?" he couldn't help asking. "There's only so many baths and massages I can spend my time on. And I'm really not used to sitting around with women, chatting about men, doing crafts and whatever else they do when they are together. I won't be very good at it."

"Is that the fate you foresee?" He shook his head. "You will be the default ambassador for your people. Our countries and cultures must learn to get along. The prima kailisa and Mele will want your knowledge and insight into Moorcondia. It's an important job, Carwyn, one that the princess would have known already, yet no one thought to school you on that role. Even after we defeat the Swarm, there could be other hostile people out there. A united front will always make us all safer."

"Oh." He hadn't considered that, and no, there hadn't been time for Nora or anyone to explain what his duties would be. He'd assumed marrying Aleki and sharing his bed was all he'd be expected to do. "I'm not certain I'm the best example of what Moorcondia has to offer."

Aleki tweaked his nipple, an act that served to arouse him more than admonish. "No one disrespects my wife like that—not even *my wife*. You are the very best of everything, my dear. I trust and love you." He punctuated the sentiment by claiming Carwyn's mouth with renewed ferocity.

As he clung to his husband, eager for him and determined to make memories that would sustain him for their long separation, Carwyn sent a silent thanks to the dowager queen. She'd known them both better than they had themselves. This was truly his destiny — this man and the life they would build together. They only had to fight for it, and together, they couldn't be stopped.

Epilogue

It was perfect weather for sailing, a small thing, yet it eased Carwyn's worry somewhat. At least his husband would be leaving under ideal conditions, even though he was heading into the worst possible ones. No one knew how long it would take to find the Swarm, let alone defeat it. He and Aleki might be old men by the time they were reunited — but he couldn't think like that. He needed to send off his husband with as much cheer as he could muster. *That is my duty and my love.* Easing Aleki's mind over the home front was the best thing he could do for him. And he absolutely couldn't think about the swing his husband had surprised him with in their home garden, just as he'd said he would all those many days ago when they'd toured the palace. The gift had caused more tears, and even more would come easily if he relived the moment.

As if thinking of him could conjure the man, there he was, striding down the dock, looking as fierce as the first time Carwyn had seen him. Only a few days ago, he'd stood in this spot saying goodbye to Cariad. That had been hard. This was worse. He put a smile on his face anyway and greeted his husband with open arms.

Aleki embraced him in a tight hug. "Thank you for being here. I know it's difficult. Seeing you as I leave port will please me very much, however."

"I won't move until your ship disappears from sight."

His husband broke the hug and replaced it with a kiss, the kind that made Carwyn's toes curl, his heart pound and his cock to rise. They'd made love countless times since their confrontation at the archery range, yet it wasn't enough. It would never be.

He shuddered and blinked back his tears as they parted by a mutual and unstated decision. They had to be strong. Many people were watching, and they needed to see their kai and his wife confident that it was not 'goodbye' so much as 'until we meet again'. Nevertheless, he indulged himself by taking Aleki's right hand in his and holding it up. His husband had made good on his promise from their wedding day and had a thin chain tattooed onto his wrist. All the world would know the man was taken. He kissed the marking and said, "Good hunting, Kai Aleki."

"Take care of my wife, Lord Carwyn."

They bowed to one another, then Aleki turned and strode back to his ship. It was the hardest thing he'd ever done, but Carwyn stayed right where he was until there was nothing left of his husband's ship to see. Then, he turned to embrace his new home.

Want to see more from this author? Here's a taster for you to enjoy!

Treaty Brides: The Secret Bride
Samantha Cayto

Excerpt

Lord Cariad of Kenworth kept his focus on the paper in front of him and ignored the busyness of the sailors around him. With the lateness of the day, the beating hot sun wasn't as much of a danger to his fair skin, and he prized any time he could take on deck. Spending most of the voyage below in the small cabin he shared with two junior officers was depressing, and the confined space was stifling. At least up here, there was a cool breeze, even if it was also populated with large men who made him uncomfortable. Not that any of them dared look sideways at him... They all believed he warmed the captain's bed, which was a ridiculous assumption, given that he was only ever in the man's cabin alone with him to go over his latest maps. He supposed men didn't need much time to fuck, although why anyone would seek an activity that made one even more sticky and sweaty was beyond him.

As he hunched over the images he etched on his paper, a shadow fell over them. He stiffened only a moment before forcing himself to relax again. "Good afternoon, Captain." He only glanced up at the man before returning his gaze to his drawing.

"What is this you do?" There was censure in the tone.

Cariad chose to ignore the disapproval. "It's important to memorialize what we find." He did look up now at the captain's stern face. "When people wonder what the fight with the Swarm was all about, drawings such as these will speak more loudly of the horror than mere words."

He gazed at his drawing again, his stomach tightening at the images he drew of the death and destruction the Swam had wrought on the small island village they'd come across the day before. Everything had been decimated, with buildings burned and bodies of mostly fighting-aged men littering the ground. The rest of the inhabitants had vanished, no doubt carried off by the Swarm to become slaves or sacrifices. Even the livestock had been slaughtered and butchered. The sight of so much savagery had haunted his thoughts and dreams all night. He had to do something to help, and this was all he could think of.

The captain grunted. "I should never have let you join my men in their exploration. It was obvious from the wrecked ships that the Swarm had been there. You are too delicate of nature to see such things."

"I appreciate your concern, sir, but I am stronger than I look." Opening the top of his lap desk, he stuck the drawing in with the rest of his sketches and closed it again, hoping it would put an end to the discussion.

The captain chuckled. "I imagine you are…with the right incentive. But soft, as well, yes? Where it counts," he added, the lecherous implication clear.

Cariad swallowed back a retort. He walked a fine line on this ship, keeping the man in charge at arm's length while not doing anything that could lead to punishment for insolence. Not that he worried overly much about his own safety... As a nobleman and cousin to the king, he was safe from any overt violence, but his work mattered. If the captain confined him to his quarters, mapping out these waters accurately would become impossible. He needed to see everything around him with a clear view to draw accurate maps.

As he'd found it useful to deflect, he asked a question that kept swirling inside his head. "Sir, how do you suppose the Swarm managed to sink so many boats?" The small island harbor had been littered with broken pieces of wood, submerged sterns and sails torn to shreds.

"I don't know." The man's tone indicated that Cariad had been successful. He was now thinking of his duty and not his loins. "I've never seen the like, and I have waged battles on the sea many times. It's disturbing. If I don't know what the danger is, I can't protect my ship and men."

A letch he may be, but the captain was good at his duty, keeping a tightly run ship with a fair yet firm hand. He hadn't been indifferent to the death and destruction his men had reported back to him. And he did appreciate the work Cariad did, praising his skill, even if he did so with a leer more often than not.

Sensing that it was a good time to take his leave, Cariad stood. "I should get washed for supper."

Ambrose's gaze slid down his body. "An excellent idea, my lord. You have sweated through your shirt."

Cariad resisted the urge to hunch his shoulders to hide the spots that stuck to the skin of his chest. He didn't understand why the sight of his skinny frame would be enticing to anyone. As far as he was concerned, he didn't have the body to interest men...or women, for that matter. He resented the fact that he was supposed to want such attention at all. "Yes, sir. I'll see you at your table later."

"Excellent. And afterward, I want you to stay with me to go over some of your most recent maps."

"As you wish, Captain." As a dance, this was getting tedious. Most every night, the man made up some reason for Cariad to stay later with him. It led to pressure on him to drink and get chummy, with the obvious goal of getting him into bed. The entire effort was tiresome, but there was no way to avoid it without causing significant resentment.

He'd taken only one step toward the hatchway when the lookout's cry sounded from his perch high up on the mast. "Ship ahoy!" Then he said something that caused Cariad's blood to freeze. "The Swarm."

There was a moment when everyone around him froze from the news. The captain was the first to leap into action. "Battle stations!" Grabbing Cariad by the shoulder, he gave him a shove. "Go to my cabin. Sean is there setting my table. Keep him with you. Bolt the door shut and don't come out, no matter what. *Now!*" he added when Cariad didn't move fast enough.

With his heart in his throat, Cariad scrambled to obey, even as his mind reeled at the sudden turn of events. He'd been out in these waters for a long time and never had they spotted a Swarm ship. They were a scouting clipper, meant to be fast and nimble. And while the crew were trained to fight, he thought they would have trouble holding their own against the vicious warriors of the Swarm. Their best hope was to outrun them. But as soon as he had that idea, there was another cry from the lookout. Cariad scanned the other side of the boat before he scrambled down the staircase and nearly stumbled at the sight of a second Swam ship heading their way.

We can't fight them both.

He had to swallow his panic as he made his way to the captain's cabin and practically threw himself through the door. Tossing his portable desk onto the floor, he turned to throw the two bolts that would only slow down any attackers. Then he stood panting as if he'd run a long distance and strained to hear what was happening up on deck.

"What's going on?" Ambrose's cabin boy, Sean, came through the archway leading to the captain's mess. His eyes were wide with fright.

Although Cariad was only a few years older than the boy, he felt responsible, not that there was anything he could do to protect him. "The Swarm have found us. There are two ships," he added, swallowing hard and looking away from the sheer terror on Sean's face now.

"We can't fight two!" the boy wailed.

"I know."

"What do we do?"

"Stay here. It's the safest place for us. And we do what we can to protect our people."

Sean wrung his hands. "How?"

"By keeping our secrets." So saying, Cariad hurried over to the captain's desk and started pulling out his own maps and the man's logs.

"Hey, you can't touch those." Sean came and reached out to stop him.

"We have to get rid of all of this before the Swarm gets their hands on it. They can't know how much we've learned. It will take away any element of surprise our fleet and the Chainers might have."

Sean's expression grew stern. "That's not for us to decide. You're only the cartographer, even if you are a lord. The captain will tan my hide if I let you destroy any of this."

Cariad was certain that the captain would have no chance to mete out any punishment. If he weren't killed outright, the man would be taken prisoner. They all would. Then they'd learn firsthand the fate of the people from the village, and all the rumors concerning the Swarm would either be confirmed or dispelled. Getting the answers wouldn't bring them any comfort. Of that, he was sure.

He opened his mouth to explain the obvious to Sean. A loud sound, followed by a rocking motion that made it hard to keep their feet under them, cut his words off. As one, he and Sean raced to the large window on the starboard side of the cabin. One of the Swarm ships had closed in on them. Smoke curled out from open ports on the side of the vessel. As Cariad squinted to see what was there, another loud sound boomed. He jumped back and collided with Sean at the sight of a large iron ball flying toward them. They both lost their footing and tumbled to the floor when their ship shuddered from what had to be an impact.

Sean clutched at his arm. "What was that? How did they make that thing fly? I didn't see a catapult."

Cariad's mind whirled to find an answer. It came to him quickly, and once more, he froze with dread. "They've weaponized fireworks."

"What?" Sean cringed against him as another explosive sound whined through the window.

Cariad held the boy in his arms for a moment to give them both comfort, little as it was. "They've found a way to create the same kind of explosion needed for fireworks and have upped the power to throw what appears to be an iron ball at us. That explains the destruction in the village harbor. They don't need the room necessary for a catapult. The balls fire straight at their target."

There was more violent rocking of the ship, and the screams of the crew as they fought to control it and save themselves were terrible. Cariad wanted to stop-up his ears, but he didn't have the luxury of giving into his terror. The outcome of the fight was obvious to him now more than ever. He had to protect his people's secrets, even as he understood that his life, one way or another, was going to be forfeit.

"Come on." He pushed Sean away, then helped him to his feet. "We need to get rid of these papers." He scrambled back to the captain's desk, struggling to stay upright as the ship trembled and swayed with each new onslaught.

"No. We can't give up hope of being victorious."

Clutching maps to his chest, Cariad rounded on the boy. "Don't be an idiot! We have already lost this battle. Soon the Swarm will board us from both sides and take anything of value before scuttling the Intrepid."

The cabin boy's lower lip wobbled, and tears pooled in his eyes. But he made no more objection, merely grabbed the captain's heavy logbook. "How do we destroy them?"

Cariad gnawed on his upper lip. Burning would be best, but there was no way to get to the galley's fire. Simply tearing the paper up wouldn't do the trick, because there wasn't time to do a proper job of it. The solution came to him then. "The privy." The captain had the luxury of having use of a hole that went straight into the sea instead of a smelly trough. It was the only course of action.

He hurried through the mess and into the privy, Sean at his heels. More explosions sent them careening into walls, but they managed to stay upright. Cariad lifted the cover and stared into the dark churning sea far below. With only a moment's hesitation, he tossed the maps he'd labored over down into the water. Then he helped Sean toss the logbook after them. They made three more trips until the captain's papers and all the maps were consigned to the ocean. There was nothing left to do except wait for their fates to play out.

The ship listed to one side, sending them onto the floor and sliding against the far wall. Through the window, they got their first look at the men of the Swarm, as they were finally boarded. Cariad closed his eyes, terrified of the nightmarish view of enormous creatures with deathly pale skin and ink-black hair. If these weren't demons, he couldn't imagine who would be.

He and Sean remained huddled together, taking as much courage as they could from each other. The sounds of a pitched battle reached their ears easily enough. It was impossible to block it out, yet worse by far was the sudden silence that told them the fighting was over. There was no doubt as to who the victors were, but it still startled him and nearly made him weep when the door shuddered from the efforts to break it open.

"Come on." Cariad staggered to his feet and helped Sean do the same. "We mustn't give them the satisfaction of seeing how scared we are."

Bold words were followed by a dry mouth and pounding heart as the wood of the door splintered from an ax. When there was a sufficiently big hole, a bloody hand was shoved through to throw the bolt. Then that same hand opened the door to let in the biggest man Cariad had ever seen. As he took in the sight of the enemy—from the long, black hair braided with beads to the stern pale face with high, slashing cheekbones and eyes that look like they glowed—he couldn't help but wonder why the gods had designed these demons with such arresting beauty. He blinked rapidly, as if he could clear what had to be a mirage. Surely the beings he feared the most couldn't cause his heart to stutter for an entirely different reason. Yet as the man approached, he had to struggle to remind himself that this was pure evil advancing on him, someone destined to make the rest of his life a miserable and probably short one.

The Swarm warrior stopped a short distance away and cocked his head as his eyes — now visibly violet in color — bore into Cariad. "Well, well, what do we have here?"

Balthazar studied the pale-haired boy standing in front of him, trying to appear brave, yet whose fear was a palpable thing. This was an intriguing development — one he couldn't keep his gaze off of. It wasn't merely his beauty, although that was stunning. More, it was the fact that he was dressed as a civilian. His companion was pretty, too, but his uniform proclaimed him a cabin boy and therefore of no real interest. Who was this well-dressed young man? Surely the Moorcondians were not so foolish as to invite the curious to join them on their scouting missions.

He took another step closer and couldn't help smiling when the boys started to take a step back, only to be brought up short by the wall behind them. "There is nowhere for you to go. Who are you?" he added, focusing his gaze on the blond-haired boy. He could practically see the thoughts turning behind those interesting eyes. They were green and gold, unlike anything he'd seen before. Quite alluring. "It's not a difficult question," he added when an answer was not forthcoming.

With a visible swallow, the boy finally replied. "I'm Cariad."

Balto chuckled. "Such a clever boy, Cariad, to know your own name. Now answer my actual question, and perhaps I need to be clearer. What are you doing on this ship? And don't say you're a cabin boy. That's what he is," he added, pointing at the quivering companion.

The one called Cariad lifted his chin in the next instant, an impressive show of courage. "It depends on your definition of what a cabin boy is. I am the captain's...doxy."

"Ah." Now here was a truly inventive answer and one that caused his cock, already hard from the battle, to jerk. It only served to pique his interest, however. Bed-warmers could be very pretty for sure, yet he doubted one would have the look of someone raised in good health and dressed in fine, if plain, clothing. His voice held tones of culture, as well, compared to the rough voices of other Moorcondians he'd encountered. This mystery made him want the boy even more and for reasons that had nothing to do with his straining cock. He could prove to be immensely useful.

He beckoned to them. "Come." When neither boy moved, he added, "You may walk to the deck on your own feet, or I and my men can sling you over our shoulders and carry you up. Your choice."

With a glare, the boy said, "That will not be necessary." He squared his shoulders and clasping the other boy's arm, moved toward the door.

Balto was almost disappointed that he wouldn't have a chance to get his hands on the enticing body. *Later.* He glared at his men in a silent command to not touch as he started to follow his captive. Something under the captain's desk caught his eye. "Stop!"

He reached down and dragged out a portable writing desk, the kind one balanced on their lap. Curious, he opened it up and had to catch the gasp of surprise before it jumped out of his mouth. The top drawings showed the destruction of their most recent pillage. A quick look through the rest of the papers showed that there were more, each one drawn with impressive detail. Here was an answer to his questions about the boy, he was sure of it.

He looked at Cariad, who stood by the door staring at him with concern. "Did you do these?"

The boy shrugged in studied indifference. "I get bored. There's nothing for me to do when the captain is otherwise occupied with his duties."

"You had to have seen this to draw it so accurately. I'm surprised the captain would allow his pretty piece of ass to wander so far away from him."

The boy's pale cheeks pinked up. "I have a vivid imagination, that's all."

"Ah. I suppose that's a good quality in a whore." When the boy dropped his gaze, he let the matter go. "Up with you, then."

He followed them to the deck, the writing desk under his arm. During his brief time below, the Moorcondians who'd survived the fight had been herded to one side to cross over onto his brother's ship — all except the captain... He kneeled in front of his new master, Malachi. The man's gaze tracked the arrival of the two boys. Sadness crossed his face and something more, as he homed in on Cariad in particular. The ship listed suddenly, testament to how much water it was taking in. It would sink quickly. Balto grabbed hold of Cariad before he tumbled backward. A shudder ran through the boy's body before he wrenched himself free. Balto let him go. There would be time enough to impose his will.

He forced himself to smile as he spoke with his brother. "Look what treasure I've found, Mal."

Malachi's attention switched from gloating over the captain to the two boys. "You always have the best of luck in that regard, Balto." He took a few steps closer. "Fresh meat is always welcome on a long voyage."

Because his brother's gaze had fixed on Cariad, Balto had to stake his claim. He grabbed the boy by the hair, anchoring him in place and ignoring the brief struggle to get free of his hold. "Indeed, and I must claim this one as my prize."

Mal sneered briefly but they'd already agreed that he would have the honor of bringing back their captives and offering the Moorcondian captain to their mother as a sacrifice. He was petty enough to want it all, yet sufficiently smart not to wage an open dispute with him. Mal was the elder of them, but Balto commanded great respect and loyalty of the men around them. "Of course. This one looks to be younger, and I bet untried." He pulled the cabin boy into his embrace by grabbing his ass. "I do love breaking them in."

"No!" The obviously terrified boy struggled to get free.

Mal put a stop to that by grasping his hair and slapping him hard. "Hold your tongue. I don't need to let you keep it to take pleasure from you." He leered into the now-crying boy's face. "You'll have to think of a way to convince me of its usefulness."

Cariad tried to lunge forward, his mouth open. Balto tugged him back and clasped a hand over those luscious lips. "Don't be stupid. You can't help him, but if you are clever, you will do as you're told and maybe you can be of use to your people after all." He kept his voice low, the words for the blond boy's ears only.

With another shudder, Cariad went still. Small tremors conveyed how hard it was for him to stay under control. He was smart, of that Balto was sure. And perhaps the boy would prove to be a gift dropped into Balto's lap, the key to solving the problem of how to put his plan in motion. It didn't do to get one's hopes up. He'd learned that harsh lesson as a boy in his own home. His long days as a marauder for his people had only reinforced that knowledge, to his bitter disappointment. The desk he clutched under his arm held the proof to how impotent he'd been so far. Maybe, by pure chance, the tide had finally turned in his favor.

Balto pushed the boy toward the railing as the ship once more warned of its impending sinking. "I am away to my ship, brother. I have all that I want from here, and I wish you a speedy return home."

"You as well, Balto, and good hunting in the meantime. When we meet again at the Citadel, I expect you to have more prizes. You know how much our illustrious mother demands her tribute. Don't disappoint her as you've been doing lately. We wouldn't want her to worry that you can't be trusted to pull your weight without me to urge you to it."

Balto bared his teeth in their way of smiling to each other, cheerfulness with a hint of menace. "Worry not, Mal. I'm setting course farther into Chain waters. Where there's one Moorcondian ship, there may be others. I look forward to engaging with a new enemy." He pushed Cariad to the planks bridging the sinking ship with his own. "Climb over and don't even think about dropping into the sea. I'd only have to go in after you, and that would make me very angry."

Cariad scowled at him. "As if I would give you the satisfaction, you monster. My people will destroy you!"

Admiring the guts of the boy, he smiled in response. "They are welcome to try. In the meantime, you're mine."

About the Author

Samantha Cayto is a Boston-area native who practices as a business lawyer by day while writing erotic romance at night—the steamier the better. She likes to push the envelope when it comes to writing about passion and is delighted other women agree that guy-on-guy sex is the hottest ever.

She lives a typical suburban life with her husband, three kids and four dogs. Her children don't understand why they can't read what she writes, but her husband is always willing to lend her a hand—and anything else—when she needs to choreograph a scene.

Samantha loves to hear from readers. You can find her contact information, website details and author profile page at https://www.pride-publishing.com

PUBLISHING

Sign up for our newsletter and find out about all our romance book releases, eBook sales and promotions, sneak peeks and FREE romance books!